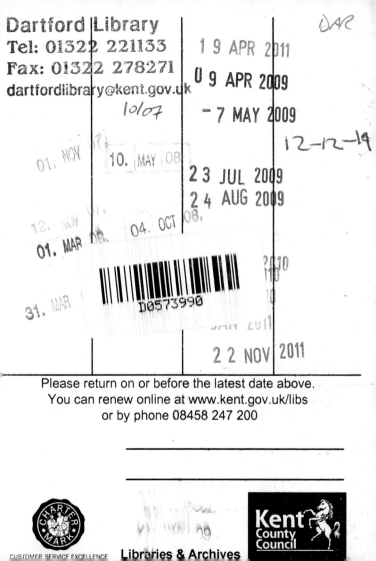

THE SPECIALIST

BY
RHONDA NELSON

MILLS & BOON

Pure reading pleasure

*All the characters in this book have no existence outside the
imagination of the author, and have no relation whatsoever to anyone
bearing the same name or names. They are not even distantly inspired
by any individual known or unknown to the author, and all the
incidents are pure invention.*

*First published in Great Britain 2007
by Harlequin Mills & Boon Limited,
Eton House, 18-24 Paradise Road, Richmond, Surrey TW9 1SR*

© Rhonda Nelson 2006

ISBN: 978 0 263 85591 3

14-1007

Harlequin Mills & Boon policy is to use papers that are
natural, renewable and recyclable products and made from
wood grown in sustainable forests. The logging and
manufacturing processes conform to the legal environmental
regulations of the country of origin.

*Printed and bound in Spain
by Litografia Rosés S.A., Barcelona*

RHONDA NELSON

A bestselling author and past RITA® Award nominee and *Romantic Times BOOKclub* Reviewers Choice nominee, Rhonda Nelson writes hot romantic comedy for the Mills & Boon® Blaze® line. In addition to a writing career, she has a husband, two adorable kids, a black Lab and a beautiful bichon frisé. She and her family make their chaotic but happy home in a small town in northern Alabama. She's secretly always had a thing for men in uniform and wouldn't object to seeing her husband in a set of dress blues.

For Jen and Vicki, my Bent Quill Posse partners
in crime, the Conference Call Queens,
Plot Wizards and friends extraordinaire.
You guys are the best.

1

FEELING A BIT LIKE a puppet master about to pull the strings, Colonel Carl Garrett shifted in his roomy first-class seat and gratefully accepted a tumbler of Kentucky bourbon from the pretty flight attendant currently smiling down at him. "Thank you," the colonel murmured.

Brian Payne, his puppet de jour and a former major under his command sat next to him, his face an impassive mask of patience…but Garrett knew better.

Payne might *appear* patient, but that was the extent of it.

In exchange for pushing Payne's end-of-service papers through—when Garrett could have just as easily made things very difficult for them—Payne and a couple of his other friends had agreed to grant him one favor. Garrett had already collected from former Major Jamie Flanagan. His lips quirked.

And he'd gotten *way* more than he bargained for.

He'd sent Flanagan to Maine to prevent his granddaughter from marrying the wrong man. Only Flanagan had ended up marrying her himself. Though that hadn't been the colonel's original intent, he had to confess that he'd been pleased with the outcome. If he'd searched the world over he couldn't have found a better man—a better partner—for his granddaughter. In seven months she'd be delivering their first child—*his* first great-grandchild—and if the child was a boy, they'd promised to name the baby after him. He didn't know when anything had delighted him as much.

Of course, if Payne succeeded on this next "favor"—and considering the man had never failed at anything in his life, Garrett had no reason to suspect that he would start now—he'd be equally delighted, though for completely different reasons. Even his recent commendation for meritorious service—his expert handling of a hostage situation, specifically—as rewarding as it was, wouldn't compare to owning a piece of history, a piece he had secretly searched for and coveted for years.

He'd let Payne stew long enough, Garrett decided. Besides, waiting the man out was a futile effort. Garrett instinctively knew he would lose.

"I'm a big Civil War buff," Garrett said conversationally, a mild understatement. He wasn't merely a "buff." According to his wife, he was obsessed, but there were worse obsessions. "Did you know that?"

Though he hadn't so much as blinked, the colonel felt Payne go on alert. "No, sir."

"Oh, yes." Garrett lifted his glass and studied the amber liquid within. "I've walked every battlefield, studied every strategy, read hundreds of letters from soldiers—mostly Confederate, of course—and even collected a few. It was a fascinating time in history," Garrett ruminated. "Fascinating time… and yet, there's no man I find more fascinating than General Robert E. Lee." Another mild understatement. Lee was brilliant, possibly the best strategist and tactician in history, American or otherwise. If he'd been able to walk the valleys of time and had the liberty to choose to meet any of the men who'd gone before him, with the exception of Jesus, Robert E. Lee would be first on his list.

Payne quirked a brow, a silent indicator which told Garrett to continue.

"Did you know he was asked to lead the Union army first, but turned it down?"

Payne inclined his head. "I seem to recall hearing that."

Garrett continued. "In a letter written to his sister, he said, 'With all my devotion to the Union and the feeling of loyalty and duty of an American citizen, I have not been able to make up my mind to raise my hand against my relatives, my children, my home.'" He sighed. "No one talks that way anymore. Lee had *passion,* Major. He was a great man."

Payne acknowledged this proclamation with the usual silent nod.

"You're going to Gettysburg," Garrett announced without further preamble.

Gratifyingly, the first notable flicker of interest sparked in Payne's annoyingly impassive gaze. "Gettysburg? What will I be doing in Gettysburg, sir?"

"I want you to find something for me."

Payne waited, presumably for him to elaborate, Garrett concluded, quite perturbed. The man was supposed to be more interested than this, dammit. Garrett frowned. It was quite unsporting of him. "Don't you want to know *what* I want you to find for me?" he asked, swallowing an impatient huff.

"I'm assuming at some point you're going to tell me, sir," he replied mildly.

Fine, Garrett thought. There was no point in playing cat and mouse with a mouse that didn't want to play. "Lee might have surrendered at Appomattox, but scholars agree the war was really lost at Gettysburg. The Confederacy never fully recovered from that defeat. Furthermore, Lee lost more than the war there. It's rumored that he lost a pocketwatch, as well."

"Rumored?" Payne repeated, seemingly interested now. "You're cashing in your favor on a *rumor?*"

It was a gamble, Garrett had to admit, but one he was willing to make. After sifting through countless letters—though none in Lee's own hand—Garrett was convinced that the watch did exist. It reportedly was engraved with the inscription "Lighthorse," meaning that it had most likely belonged to Lee's father, Harry.

If it existed—and he thought it did—then Garrett wanted it.

And if anyone could find it, then Brian Payne—aka The Specialist—could.

Operating on the belief that the watch had never made it out of Gettysburg, Garrett had kept feelers out at various antique dealers and pawn shops over the years. Up to this point they'd yielded frustrating leads which had inevitably arrived at dead ends. But now Garrett thought he'd finally received a viable clue. He scowled.

Unfortunately, so had another rival collector.

And unfortunately this rival collector was also a friend, one who'd had the nerve to bet him— only one of many wagers over the years—that his rebel rule-bending girl could find it before Garrett's Specialist could.

Hogwash.

Granted, Garrett knew enough about Emma Langsford and her service in the military not to completely discount her. But to consider her a worthy opponent to Payne? One of his Project Chameleon protégés? Hell, Payne had been part of a secret unit that couldn't be found in any file, computer-generated or otherwise. He and his friends had been *the best*. So, would Emma Langsford be a match for Payne? He thought not.

Since Emma had recently left the service, as well, Garrett imagined that he wasn't the only person cashing in a favor, so to speak. No doubt

Emma owed Colonel Martin Hastings, as well. He couldn't imagine any other reason the woman would agree to go and look for the watch.

Garrett had debated whether or not to tell Payne about Emma, but ultimately decided against it. In the first place, Payne needed to stay focused and if he was worrying about keeping up or even one step ahead of the woman, then he wouldn't be able to properly utilize that eerily pragmatic brain of his.

And secondly, somehow he didn't think Payne would appreciate being the object of a bet between friends. He'd undoubtedly take exception to his manipulated part in this wager. Naturally Garrett wanted to win, but he wanted the watch more.

Luckily, he had every confidence that he'd have both.

"I have what I believe is a solid lead in Gettysburg," Garrett finally continued. "According to a local auctioneer, a watch with the same inscription as what's rumored to be on the one Lee lost at Gettysburg was recently sold in the estate sale of an elderly woman who was an avid collector of, well…junk. She most likely didn't know what she had."

"What was the inscription?"

"Lighthorse, after Lee's—"

"Father," Payne finished, displaying a gratifying knowledge of Confederate history. "So if you know it was sold at auction, then there should be a record of who bought it and for how much. You shouldn't need me to go find it."

Garrett grimaced. Yes, he'd originally thought it was going to be that simple, as well. "Evidently this was a slipshod job and most of the items were sold in lots. The woman owned dozens of watches and they were sold off in groups of three."

Payne sat there for a moment, seemingly absorbing what Garrett had just shared. Predictably, he came to the same conclusion Garret himself had. "So the watch—provided it even exists—could be *anywhere*."

Exactly, Garrett thought. He looked away and quaffed the rest of his bourbon. "I'm confident you can find it."

Then that made only one of them, Payne thought, resisting the pressing urge to grind his teeth. Given the nature of Jamie's favor, Payne had known that trying to anticipate Garrett's next request was an effort in futility. But he had to admit, never in a million years would he have expected Garrett to send him on a freaking treasure hunt for a fabled pocketwatch.

One that had supposedly belonged to Robert E. Lee.

And which may or may not even exist.

It was madness. Payne inwardly frowned. And it was going to be extremely time-consuming.

"If it exists, then I will find it," Payne said, bristling at having his Ranger training squandered on such a frivolous task. "However, I cannot afford to devote more than a week away from work." It wasn't altogether true, he supposed, but Jamie had set a precedent and frankly, Garrett wasn't getting any more out of him than absolutely necessary. He'd agreed to one favor and he would deliver to the best of his ability. It was not in his character to do otherwise. But clearly the colonel had been on this quest for many years and Payne had no intention of getting sucked into an indefinite search.

"I'm a reasonable man, Payne. If you can't find it within a week, then you can give me what information you've gathered up to that point and I'll take it from there."

Fair enough, Payne thought. For reasons he couldn't begin to explain, he got the distinct impression that the colonel was holding out on him. "Is there anything else I should know, sir?" he asked, more to gauge Garrett's response than to mine for a real answer.

"Just this," Garrett replied after a slight hesitation. He pulled a folder from his briefcase and handed it to him. "This has the necessary information. Contacts, a map of the area, your plane ticket and reservation. I've booked you into a bed and breakfast rather than a hotel. You get better service at a B&B and the owners are generally more informed about local history. This particular one is called The Dove's Nest and has been in the same family for several generations. Oral history is becoming a forgotten art, but by all accounts this family is one of the better-informed in the area."

Be that as it may, Payne figured he'd have more anonymity at a hotel than a B&B. Furthermore, what about modern conveniences? He had no desire whatsoever to share a bathroom with anyone and he grimly suspected he'd be forced to depend upon a dial-up connection versus the high-speed cable version he could expect from even the cheapest hotel chain. But because he'd mastered the art of keeping his emotions completely in check—it was easier to keep a potential threat from using them against him—Payne didn't so much as grimace at this idea, though internally his organs were beginning to twist with dread.

He did not want to do this.

It was a pointless waste of time—*his* time—because if the damned pocketwatch existed at all, he was certain some other Civil War Robert E. Lee buff would have snatched it up ages ago, displaying it for other Civil War Robert E. Lee buffs to salivate over.

Though many collectors would probably state otherwise, the purpose of possessing items worthy of collecting wasn't to satisfy some personal need, but to showcase what other collectors wanted but couldn't have. A cynical view? Probably. But it was his opinion and he was entitled to it.

Furthermore, that telling pause he'd noticed when he'd probed for more information told him that Garrett wasn't being completely honest with him. Something else was at work here. He didn't doubt that the colonel wanted the watch. Clearly adding it to his cache of Confederate memorabilia would be a coup. But he wanted something else, as well.

The million-dollar question, of course, was… what?

Oh, hell. What did it matter? Payne thought, his lips curling into a vague smile. So long as he wasn't guarding another granddaughter, he should thank his lucky stars. Women, he knew from personal experience, tended to complicate things and he'd just as soon avoid complications.

And since women and complications tended to go hand in hand, other than to scratch an occasional itch, he typically avoided them, as well.

Too much trouble, too little reward, too little time.

Women tended to make the men in his family do stupid things, like forego prenuptial agreements and crash their cars and drink too much. They made them miserable and weak and out of control. And for what? Good sex? A handy dinner companion? Another body in the bed? He smirked. Hell, he could get all of that free, usually in the course of one night. And, other than paying the tab for a meal, his finances were still in good standing, as well as his pride.

Payne had watched both of his parents barter their self-respect for love to the point where he wondered how they could face themselves in the mirror each morning. He certainly couldn't respect them, that was for damned sure. All he felt was pity and contempt, limited fond memories of a lonely childhood and a snarled-up obligation toward his parents he wished he could let go of.

Both Guy and Jamie—his brothers of the heart, comrades and current business partners—called him a cynic, but what the hell.

Being a cynic was better than being stupid any day.

2

"SO WHAT ARE WE SELLING next? The fine china or the Fabergé egg collection?"

Emma Langsford smiled at the comment and shook her head, but didn't look up from the scarred desk in her mother's beauty shop where she was currently working on the books. A piercing throb had developed behind her right eye and an empty hollow feeling of dread had commenced in her belly.

It felt like she was...*broke.*

Unfortunately, she recognized the feeling all too well.

Point of fact, in an effort to keep the bank from foreclosing on the family home, they'd sold off everything that hadn't been deemed an absolute necessity months ago. Continuing care for her grandfather until his death had been a huge drain on her mother's already strained finances and it had taken every last penny in her mother's woeful collection to make sure that her grandfather hadn't suffered. Cancer, Emma thought bitterly. Damned miserable disease.

Rather than re-up for another four years in the military, as much as they'd needed what little money she could send home, Emma had left the army and had returned to Marble Springs to be there for her mother. Lena Evans might have needed money, but when going through the final stages of losing her father, she'd needed her daughter more.

Unfortunately, aside from coming home and helping her mother, Emma hadn't made any additional plans. She'd gone to work at the local grocery store to help make ends meet, and planned to cash in on her military service for college. But unless a windfall landed in their lap, she couldn't see being able to enroll anytime soon. Emma had a reputation for making rash decisions, but usually she managed to come out on top. She frowned.

In this instance, she'd definitely landed sideways.

"We're not going to sell anything else, Mom. There's nothing left to sell." With the exception of her body, that is, Emma thought with a grim smile.

But as much as she loved the old home-place, she wasn't willing to make that sort of sacrifice. At least…not yet. She reached down and absently stroked Moses's patchy furr, feeling as much like the stray as the old dog who'd adopted her immediately upon her return home. "I'm going to see if I can pick up some extra work."

With her shears poised over Mrs. Wilkins's smoky-blue hair, her mother stilled and stared at her. "More work? Absolutely not. You're already picking up every hour of overtime you can at the store and I know that you've been going over helping Darcy Marcus at This Bud's For You."

Damn. "She needed help pulling a few arrangements together for Decoration Day."

He mother glared at her. "Darcy Marcus made your life a living hell all through school. She made fun of your clothes, purposely excluded you from every party and what about the prom? She hijacked your date!"

Emma grimaced. All true, still… "He wasn't much of a date to start with."

"Be that as it may, you don't have to work for *her.*"

Emma had known her mother would react that way—that's why she hadn't mentioned the extra work with Darcy. But honest work was honest work. She'd also picked up a couple of cover shifts at the video store for Dwight Allen. Dwight had stolen her peanut butter and jelly sandwich in kindergarten, but that hadn't kept her from working for him, either.

They were too poor to be too proud and as long as she was off the street corner and someone was willing to pay her to do honest work, she'd do it. Hell, she'd made it through basic training and had thrived in the military. She could withstand a little degrading company in exchange for the cash they needed. Was it galling? Of course. She wouldn't be human if she hadn't felt that way. But Emma had to keep the greater good of things in mind, and if that meant swallowing a little pride in order to put food on the table, then that's what she'd do.

"Well, I don't care how bad we need the money, we'll sell the Victrola before you work another minute for Darcy Marcus."

"Ouch!" Mrs. Wilkins yelped with an angry glance up at Lena. "You're pulling my hair."

"Sorry," her mother mumbled contritely.

"We're not selling the Victrola," Emma said, repressing a weary sigh. That Victrola had belonged to her grandparents and represented the last bastion of a life that they used to know. Even Emma could remember her grandparents breaking the old album player out, moving the furniture back against the walls and dancing around the living room. There were dozens of happy memories associated with the old piece and she would not—*absolutely could not*—let it go.

They'd lose the house before they lost the Victrola.

"Emmaline," her mother began, using her full given name. "I want you to promise me that you won't—"

Thankfully the telephone rang, cutting off the beginning of an extorted promise Emma had no intention of keeping.

"Lena's On Main," Emma answered.

"Emma?" asked a familiar voice, one she'd never expected to hear again.

"Colonel Hastings?"

"Ah, it is you," he said happily.

She sincerely doubted her old boss needed a hair cut or a manicure, so to say that his call was unexpected would have been a huge understatement. "Er…yes, sir. It's me."

"Excellent, Langsford. I have a business proposition I'd like to run by you and I wondered if you were available at the moment to talk."

"Sure, sir," Emma told him, struggling to keep her jaw from hitting the floor.

"Excellent. I'm outside in the black town car. I'll wait for you."

Flabbergasted, Emma felt her eyes widen. She craned her head toward the front of the store and peered out the window. *Colonel Hastings was here? In Marble Springs? But—*

"Is something wrong?" her mother asked, evidently noting the shocked look on her daughter's face.

"Er… I'll be right out, sir." Emma replaced the receiver, then stood and glanced distractedly at her mother. "Colonel Hastings is here."

Lena's perfectly arched brows furrowed. "Colonel Hastings? But isn't that—"

"It is," Emma confirmed grimly.

"Well, what does he want?"

Now, that was an excellent question, Emma thought as she made her way to the door. She had absolutely no idea.

Emma ordered Moses to stay—he followed her *everywhere,* bless his old grateful heart—then slid her suddenly sweating palms over her thighs, pushed through the door and out into the biting winter air. Exhaust streamed from the muffler of the town car idling at the curb. The rear passenger window powered down, revealing the colonel's smiling face. "Ah," he said. "Now aren't you a sight for sore eyes. Come on, child." He opened the door for her. "Climb on in."

Still a bit rattled by his unexpected visit, Emma slid into the roomy back seat and savored the warmth which instantly enveloped her. The heat in her old Ford had played out and she was typically an icicle before she made it into town.

"It's, er… It's nice to see you sir," she finally managed to say for lack of anything better. A more relevant response would have been "What the hell are you doing here?" but she couldn't see herself asking that question.

Not to him.

"Oh, and you, too," he said, looking as though he really meant it.

She knew that he'd had high hopes for her and that he'd been disappointed when she'd decided to leave the military, but… Well, she never dreamed he'd actually look her up.

"Is there a café or anything nearby where we could talk?" he asked.

"Sure. There's a little diner up on the corner."

The colonel instructed the driver to take them there, then turned once more to her and smiled. "I'm sure you have to be wondering what I'm doing here."

Emma felt a grin twist her lips. "I'll admit I'm a little curious," she said lightly.

"Such cheek," he enthused, seemingly charmed. "That's what I always liked about you, Langsford. Wit, courage, smarts. You should have stuck with me. You had a promising career."

Emma swallowed. "I know, sir. I—"

"No worries," he interrupted soothingly. "We all do what we have to do," he said. "I understood it then and I understand it now. That's part of the reason I'm here."

Now, that was certainly an enigmatic comment, Emma thought, growing increasingly intrigued as to the reason for the colonel's visit.

Five minutes later they were ensconced in a scarred booth with patched vinyl seats. Curiously, though she wouldn't have thought it possible, the colonel looked right at home. He calmly sampled his coffee, smiled at the overweight waitress who delivered the brew and idly glanced around the room, seemingly charmed by the worn decor.

"So this is home," he said. "Quaint, but nice. I can see why you'd want to come back here."

Emma nodded. Granted there were lots of things about Marble Springs which got on her nerves—the busybodies minding everyone's business, for starters—but overall it was a nice town. Three generations of her family had been born and raised here. There was something to be said for that kind of heritage. Roots, Emma decided. Roots were important.

"Sir, I don't mean to be disrespectful, but... why are you here?"

He smiled. "And that's another thing I always liked about you. You're direct."

As nice as this all was, she'd really appreciate it if he'd get to the point. "You said you had a business proposition for me? What sort of proposition?"

He finally leaned forward in his seat, a silent indicator that he was ready to get down to business, the business that had evidently brought him all the way from Fort Benning, Georgia, to her little Mississippi town, population five thousand. "Since you appreciate directness, Langsford, I'm going to get right to the point."

Emma nodded, encouraging him to go on.

"There's a piece of Confederate history which has recently surfaced in Gettysburg and I want you to go get it for me."

Emma frowned. Why did he need her to go and get it? Why couldn't he do it himself?

"The whereabouts are a bit murky," he said, evidently anticipating her next question, "and it's going to take someone with your…particular set of skills to acquire it for me."

"My set of skills?" she asked.

"Precisely. You're quick, you're uncannily lucky and, when you want something, you're ruthless."

Emma internally recoiled. She wasn't *ruthless,* damn it—she was determined. There was a difference. Granted, it might be subtle, but it *was* there. Had other people seen her that way? she wondered, suddenly alarmed. Had her comrades thought she was ruthless? She'd always been competitive, but ruthless?

"Sir, I think—"

"And when I finish telling you about this mission, Langsford," he continued, warming to his topic, "you're going to want it. Badly."

"Want what?"

"The pocketwatch I'm sending you after."

Emma resisted the urge pull out her hair. "Pocketwatch?"

"This particular pocketwatch belonged to General Robert E. Lee. I want it. In fact, I want it so badly that I have bet a fellow officer—a fellow collector—that you can get to it first. Before his guy can."

Patience had been a virtue she'd always lacked, so as much as she respected the colonel, Emma didn't mince any words. "Sir, this makes absolutely no sense. I, uh— I don't have time to look for a pocketwatch, whether it belonged to Robert E. Lee or not. And frankly, I have too much to do and too much to worry about to discuss this any furth—"

"Ten thousand dollars," he said calmly.

Emma drew up short. "I'm sorry?"

"That's what I'm willing to pay you."

"Pay me?" she squeaked.

"That's right. If *you* get to the watch first and deliver it to *me,* I will pay *you* ten thousand dollars."

Emma chewed the inside of her cheek, leaned back into the seat and regarded him seriously for the first time since this bizarre conversation began. She could do a lot with ten thousand dollars. *Satisfy the back taxes, take care of the mortgage. Start school.* "Brief me again, sir. Please."

He did. "You will have an advantage because I'm relatively certain that Garrett didn't share the terms of the bet—or even mention it, for that matter—to Major Payne. Are you familiar with him?"

Emma felt a flutter wing through her belly. Blond hair, ice blue eyes, a body any warm-blooded woman would instantly salivate over. He was aloof and legendary, supposedly untouchable. Her mouth parched. Oh, yeah. "I've heard of him."

"He's a strong opponent, but you'll have an edge. You know that he's after the same thing that you are…but he isn't aware of any competition. Beautiful, isn't it?"

In order to beat him to it, Emma knew she'd need every advantage she could get. Granted she knew her own worth—she *was* quick, she *was* good—but Payne had a reputation for being equally good…if not better. And since Emma now knew what she was up against—and how desperately Hastings wanted to insure her participation as well as his victory—she decided different terms were in order.

"Ten now, plus expenses," Emma said. "And ten upon delivery." That was the magic number. She could take care of the back taxes, satisfy what was left on the mortgage and get a jump-start on school. She might be young, but she wasn't stupid. She needed this. It was exactly the kind of opportunity she'd needed to put her and her mother's life back on track.

The colonel chuckled. "You want to bargain? What makes you think you're in a position to bargain?"

Emma smiled at him and cocked her head. "You tipped your hand the instant you drove over here, sir. You need me as much as I need your money."

Hastings guffawed, a giant belly laugh which made other diners glance over at them. "And that's the sort of deduction that makes you worth it. Consider it done, Langsford. I've got the necessary paperwork in the car. You leave tomorrow. I trust that won't be a problem?"

She'd have to cancel on Darcy, but that was actually a bonus. Emma brightened. A secret thrill whipped through her. A mission. Now this was more like it. "Not at all, sir."

"Excellent. I have your ticket, but you'll need to take care of hotel accommodations."

Emma nodded, her heart lightened with a newfound hope, one she hadn't had in a long, long time. "Is there anything else I should know about, sir?"

The colonel leveled a grave stare at her. "Major Payne isn't called The Specialist for nothing. He'll play by the rules." He shrugged and a crafty gleam suddenly lit his ordinarily jovial gaze. "Let's just say you don't have to."

So in other words, he wanted her to do whatever she had to do to get it first. Emma felt a wry smile roll around her lips.

And *she* was supposedly ruthless?

3

"THIS IS BULLSHIT," Guy said in his usual blunt fashion. "I can't believe you've agreed to do this."

Payne collected his bags from the trunk of Guy's car and set them on the curb. Rather than leave his SUV parked in the dubious care of airport security, Payne had asked Guy to give him a ride this morning. If he hadn't needed to pack another bag and take care of a few niggling business details, he could have gotten off the plane with Garrett and immediately hopped on another toward Gettysburg. But he'd needed a few hours to pull things together for a week's absence. "We all agreed, remember?"

"We agreed to do a favor, just a favor. Don't you think this is a tad over the top? First, a flirting mission for Jamie, now a freakin' treasure hunt for you?" Guy snorted. "What's next?"

Payne chuckled and shot his friend a you-poor-bastard look. "That'll be your problem, won't it?"

Guy grimaced, rubbed a hand over the back of his neck. "I'd be lying if I said I wasn't nervous. This is… This is ridiculous, even for Garrett."

"We gave our word." And no matter how futile paying back this favor might seem, it was still worth it. Getting out of the military had been the best thing for all three of them.

"I know that, dammit," Guy snapped. "I'm not balking. I'm just annoyed." He passed a hand over his face, then smiled. "At least I don't have to worry about you running off, getting married and becoming a seasonal worker."

Payne almost smiled. "Definitely not."

Though Jamie was still a partner and participated in the day-to-day operations at Ranger Security, he did it from a significant distance. The business was based in Atlanta and Jamie had recently taken up residence in Maine. His new wife's business was headquartered there and, while Jamie would never admit it for fear of being thought of as henpecked, both Payne and Guy knew that Jamie preferred the quiet shores of Lake Bliss to the bustling city of Atlanta. In fact, it was quite obvious that their friend, the ultimate former player, was happier with Audrey Kincaid Flanagan than he'd ever been with anyone in his life.

Payne and Guy had teased him ruthlessly about it, of course, because they'd formed a pact in college to remain bachelors. They'd even come up with three hard and fast rules to resist the possible temptation of falling in love. One, never let a woman eat off your plate. Two, never spend the whole night with her and three, after the third date cut her loose.

Jamie had succumbed to all three a few months ago, and typical of a newly shackled man, was happily imagining Payne and Guy's downfall, as well. "You'll see," he'd told them. "You pitying bastards think you've got it all worked out. You don't. When the right woman comes along, she's gonna blow those rules out of the water and you're not going to know what's hit you. Believe me, I know," he predicted direly.

He couldn't speak for Guy, of course, but Payne knew beyond a shadow of a doubt that there wasn't a woman alive who could knock him so far off his game he'd *marry* her. He wasn't so arrogant to think that he might never be tempted into falling in love—he wouldn't tempt Fate by even thinking something like that—but he knew himself and his own resolve well enough to know that he damned sure wasn't going to permanently attach himself in front of God and witnesses and, most important, the court, to one.

Frankly, he had better sense.

Granted, marriage definitely seemed to be suiting Jamie, but he and Jamie were two completely different people. Despite Jamie's previous stint in serial dating, Payne had always detected a bit of a longing for a family in Jamie.

When Danny, their good friend and comrade, had died in their last covert mission for Uncle Sam, things had only worsened for Jamie. Understandably, of course, considering that Danny had taken his last breath in Jamie's arms. He and Guy hadn't known that unfortunate tidbit until recently, but once they'd found it out, many of the things that Jamie had done—withdrawing from them, going through girls like water—had begun to make sense.

That was the only thing about Danny's death that made any sense, though, Payne thought as a familiar pang of loss squeezed his chest. Getting out of the military had become a mission in and of itself after that had happened, which was why they'd all landed themselves in Garrett's debt to start with. They'd been provoked into a barroom brawl—off-base, no less—by an arrogant ass who'd mouthed off about their fallen friend. The incident could have held up their clearance papers indefinitely, but Garrett had found a way to push them through.

His price, of course, had been a favor—from each of them.

Payne released a small breath. That was why he now found himself packed and ready to go to Gettysburg in search of a freaking pocketwatch Garrett only *thought* existed and apparently wanted badly enough to send him to get it. Civil War buff? Hell, the man was obsessed.

And though he was a former Ranger, not an errand boy, Payne's word was his word. Growing up in an unstable home where he heard more lies than truths, Payne valued honesty and structure above all else. Did he like Garrett's request? No. But it didn't change the fact that he owed him.

Payne shouldered his garment bag, grabbed his laptop case and turned to face Guy. "Call me if anything comes up."

"We'll be fine," Guy assured him. "Jamie and Audrey are flying in tomorrow."

Since Audrey's season at Unwind—her de-stressing camp for burned-out execs, harried mothers and the like—was officially over, she and

Jamie were going to act like snowbirds and head south for the winter. Or at least part of it, at any rate. Jamie would work here on-site until Audrey's season started again, then they'd head north once more. "I've offered them my loft for the week," Payne told him.

Guy closed the trunk. "Jamie told me. They're going to go ahead and move their stuff into my place. A lot of Jamie's things are still there, and they didn't want to go through the hassle of moving downstairs once you got back. You're fine with that, right?"

Payne nodded, secretly relieved. He preferred his privacy and, while he knew there was nothing in his loft he didn't mind them seeing, he still wasn't altogether comfortable having anyone in his space. It was odd, he knew. He'd certainly shared more than an apartment with these guys over the years. Still…

"I'll be in touch," Payne finally told Guy, dreading this with every fiber of his being, but anxious to get it over with nonetheless. The sooner he found the watch—or didn't, whatever the case may be—the sooner he could get back to Atlanta and work. While he'd enjoyed his time in the military, Payne had to confess that he'd slipped into civilian mode without incident. Structure was structure no matter where one put it into practice, he supposed.

Guy chuckled. "Happy hunting."

"Smart-ass."

"Hey, while you're up there, why don't you see if you can find the Holy Grail, as well?"

Payne chewed the inside of his cheek to keep from smiling. "Your time's coming," he reminded him. "Remember that."

Guy winced, suddenly serious. "Trust me. I'm not likely to forget."

He supposed not, Payne thought. And considering what Garrett had put him and Jamie through, Guy had every reason to worry. God only knew what sort of favor he'd ask of him.

To hell with it, Payne thought, making his way into the terminal. He just wanted it to be over.

And the sooner the better.

EMMA DUTIFULLY CALLED her mother the instant she deplaned to let Lena know she'd arrived without incident. She was shoving her cell phone back into her bag when she suddenly collided with something big, hard and warm…and were it not for the equally big, warm hands clamped upon her upper arms, she would have toppled gracelessly to the ground.

After emitting a very unladylike grunt, followed by a stinging curse, she looked up into the face of her savior and wished that she *had* fallen.

Directly into a black hole.

Cool winter blue eyes stared down at her and the hint of a smile lurked on a pair of lips which instantly made her think of slow deep kisses and hot frantic sex. She'd seen his mouth from a distance, of course—like the rest of him—but this up close and personal view was wreaking havoc in places that hadn't had so much as a mild uprising in over a year. A warm tingle started in her midsection and radiated outward until it zinged into hot spots which would undoubtedly love his carnal mouth's singularly focused attention.

He had a reputation for being cool, detached, focused, methodical and foolproof and Emma would be lying if she hadn't nursed a crush of sorts, a secret fantasy of being on the receiving end of that sort of…undivided attention. He wouldn't merely *seduce,* he would *consume,* and the idea of being overcome by the mysteriously aloof Brian Payne was almost more than she could handle.

It was unnerving. She'd expected to run into him in the course of her quest, but she hadn't expected it to be in the *literal* sense.

At the airport, no less.

Still, she thought, reminding herself to breathe, this wasn't necessarily a bad thing. She knew he hadn't gotten the jump on her, for starters.

"I'm s-sorry," Emma finally stammered awkwardly. She drew back, righting her purse and carry-on bag.

"No problem," he told her, that cool gaze assessing her, causing little hot-flashes to blink in rhythm to a mental warning light. "You're not hurt, I hope."

Emma felt a sheepish grin tug at her lips. "The only thing aching at the moment is my pride, but it'll recover."

The comment drew a vague smile. "You look familiar," he said, seemingly trying to place her. "Have we met?"

Mildly panicked, Emma shook her head. "Er…no, we haven't," she answered truthfully. They *hadn't* been formally introduced…but they might have met in passing once or twice.

"My mistake, then."

"Er…well, thank you for catching me," she said, deciding it was time to end this little chat. She readjusted her bags, and started to move around him. "I appreciate it."

"No problem."

Before he could puzzle anymore over where he might have seen her, Emma made her way down the concourse. She could feel his gaze boring into her back and knew that he was only a few paces behind her without looking over her shoulder to see—she could *feel* him. She determinedly ignored the prickly sensation tingling at the nape of her neck, the restless heat suddenly swelling below her belly button and forced herself to think of something else.

The money did the trick.

She needed it too badly to let herself get side-tracked by a set of cool blue eyes and impossibly wide shoulders.

Since she hadn't checked any baggage—she'd managed to cram an entire week's bulky winter wardrobe into her carry-on bag—she avoided baggage claim and made her way past the luggage carousels, directly to the car rental counter. From the corner of her eye she watched Payne snag a single black suitcase from the conveyer, then scan the various rental company signs until he found the one he wanted.

Unfortunately, it was hers.

Shit.

Another one of those almost-but-not-quite implied smiles haunted his lips as he sauntered toward her. "We meet again," he said. A gratifying flash of appreciation flared in those wintry eyes.

Emma managed a weak grunt, which she was sure matched her equally weak smile. She wanted to have a general idea of his whereabouts and what he was up to, but having him tail her gave him too many opportunities to try to place her. Given his reputation, she knew if he made the connection it wouldn't take long for him to figure the whole thing out. Then the one advantage she'd had would be lost.

And that would be bad.

Rather than wait for the clerk to ask for her name, Emma pulled out her ID and handed it to him before he could ask. "I'm in a bit of a hurry," she said, hoping to spur the guy along.

"Certainly." He scanned his computer screen, then winced. "You reserved a sedan. Unfortunately, we've overbooked and only have a couple of vehicles left."

Emma tamped down her initial irritation, felt Payne's interest shift from her to the car rental clerk. "What do you have left?" she asked, pleased that her voice didn't climb right along with her blood pressure.

He stroked a few keys, focusing on the computer screen. "Looks like we've got an H2 and—" He peered at the monitor, then looked up at her and grinned, showing enough metal in his mouth to power a small country. "And a VW Bug. How about I put you in that one?"

Emma's initial reaction was to say yes, the Bug would be fine. Truth be told, she'd always thought they were adorable and, if she'd been able to afford a new car, the VW was definitely what she'd want. But something about the clerk's automatic assumption that she wouldn't want—or couldn't handle—the Hummer pricked a nerve. Furthermore, while the idea of her behind the wheel of the Bug was appealing, the idea of putting Payne behind it was even more so. She felt an evil smile tease her lips and had to forcibly resist the urge to look at him.

Emma cleared her throat. "What happens to my rate?" she asked. She had to be practical, after all. "Will it go up?"

He shook his head. "No, not since we weren't able to accommodate your initial reservation."

Emma smiled brightly. "In that case, I'll take the Hummer."

Though he hadn't so much as moved a muscle, Emma could feel Payne's displeasure bouncing off her, pinging her like sonar. Though it could only be her imagination, the temperature in the room seemed to plummet.

Evidently the clerk felt it, too, because his chromelike smile faltered. "It's an awfully big ride, ma'am," he said, giving her a quick once over. "Are you sure you wouldn't be more comfortable in the Bug?"

Yes, she probably would. But Payne would be more *un*comfortable in the Bug and, at the moment, Payne's discomfort was a lot more appealing. Furthermore, she might be small, but she was more than capable of handling the Hummer. She mentally rolled her eyes. Hell, it couldn't be any more difficult than manning a tank.

"I'm sure," Emma told him. "In this instance, *size matters*," she said, and thought she heard a little choked noise beside her. She winced, hoping to pull off a little vulnerability. "I'd feel *safer* in the Hummer."

"Of course," he said, albeit reluctantly. He expelled a small breath and, looking as though he knew the coming exchange with his next customer was going to be unpleasant, printed out the necessary paperwork and handed her the keys. "I'll let them know that you're coming," he said, indicating the outside staff.

Emma grinned, snagged the keys and turned to leave. Her gaze tangled with Payne's and the commingled flash of irritation, suspicion and grudging admiration she saw in those twin blue pools made her belly tip in a wild roll. He knew what she'd done—that she'd *purposely* chosen the Hummer to thwart him—and it suddenly occurred to Emma that her petty act of unwarranted revenge might have thrown up a red flag.

In front of a legendary bull, no less.

Oy.

"Drive safely," he murmured silkily as she walked past, his voice laced with an edge of menace that she found curiously thrilling.

Never one to allow herself to be intimidated, Emma merely cocked a brow. "You, too," she said. Then without sparing him another glance, she walked away, her stomach trembling.

4

PAYNE ORDINARILY DIDN'T make rash decisions. He was practical, methodical, focused—he relied on an economy of logic to lead him to his actions and decisions. This was his modus operandi, his preferred method of operation and yet one provoking slightly self-satisfied look and a cat-in-the-cream-pot smile from a hot little crackerjack of a female had totally thrown him off his game.

Why else would he have decided to rent the Bug—when he could have just as easily gone to another car rental counter and gotten something more suitable?

It was the height of illogical stupidity, and yet he couldn't seem to help himself. There'd been something vaguely familiar about her when she'd plowed into him on the concourse. Certainly he'd never been introduced to her—there's no way he would have forgotten those eyes.

They were unforgettable.

Deep blue, the shade of sugared violets and fringed with long, curly lashes. He'd kept her from falling, but only by sheer force of will had he kept his own feet beneath him when she'd looked up and her startled gaze had connected with his.

Payne wasn't accustomed to being shocked. Little if anything ever produced more than a ripple over the calm pond of his composure. He prided himself on his generally unerring ability to keep his emotions in check, on never losing control. It was the source of his strength, irrefutable proof that he wouldn't be like his weak-willed father or his impetuous, unpredictable mother.

To his immense discomfort and surprise, however, one look into the eyes of his mystery Hummer woman had done more than merely shake him up—she'd rocked his very foundation. Only an idiot would go after her, Payne thought as he scanned the line of rental vehicles, his gaze instantly alighting on her shapely rear as she climbed into the driver's seat.

He muttered a curse under his breath. She damn near needed a step ladder to get in the bloody SUV. At six and a half feet, Payne was used to being taller than most everybody, but he wasn't just *taller* than her—he *towered* over her. She couldn't be more than five one or two—he could easily pick her up with one hand—but what she lacked in height she more than made up for with attitude. An unwelcome flash of heat engulfed his loins, forcing him to clench his jaw.

And sex appeal.

He'd never had what one could call a prefer-ence when it came to what attracted him to the opposite sex, but whatever it was, this woman—whoever *she* was—had it in spades. She had short, black tousled-looking curls, those amazing eyes which had sucked the wind right out of his lungs, small elfinlike features—high cheekbones, a rather sharp nose and lips that put a man in mind of a ripe strawberry—and a strength of character, determination and the smallest hint of vulnerabil-ity which he instinctively knew she'd resent. She was small, but curvy and fit and, despite her petite size, she'd felt curiously right in his arms a few moments ago.

In a word, she was fascinating.

He'd spent a combined total of five minutes in her company and was so thoroughly intrigued that he'd allowed himself to be put into a VW Bug—a lime green one, no less, dammit, Payne realized as his gaze zeroed in on the little car. Ironically, it was parked directly in front of the Hummer and looked as if it was waiting to get squashed. His lips quirked.

Furthermore, given the way the mystery woman precisely angled the mirrors, she looked strangely capable of doing the job herself, he thought, reluctantly impressed. She didn't look the least bit apprehensive or worried about handling the monster-sized vehicle.

Payne's grim gaze slid to the Bug once more. He wasn't worried about handling it, per se. What he *was* concerned about was fitting into the damned thing.

Ultimately, that's what had put her so firmly on his radar.

Payne was pretty good at reading people, prided himself on his ability to size a person up. It had been a handy tool as a Ranger and, curiously, even handier in the private sector. He could easily discern a lie from the truth, knew when a prospective client was seeking his services for a dishonorable or legitimate cause. That keen ability had kept Ranger Security out of less desirable jobs and off the payroll of more than one unscrupulous character.

When the car rental clerk had announced that he only had a couple of cars left, naturally Payne had gone on alert. He'd had a vested interest, after all, and it behooved him to pay close attention. As such, he'd watched her closely to see which car she would choose. She'd wanted the Bug—he'd known from the quick flash of wistfulness he'd seen in those remarkable eyes—and yet she'd ultimately chosen the Hummer.

A wicked, gleeful glint had sparked to life in her gaze—detectable even from his profiled vantage point, and he'd realized with a start of his recently dulled insight that she'd chosen it simply to keep him from having it.

He'd been shocked again. Twice within the space of a few minutes.

He was a stranger, ostensibly someone whom she would have no desire to thwart or inconvenience…but she had. And she'd enjoyed it too much for it to have been mere coincidence. An interesting truth evolved from that line of thinking, one that piqued his interest and put him instantly on guard. He might find her only vaguely familiar, but she *knew* him.

Which begged a million questions, the most pressing of which was, from where?

Considering he'd only been in Atlanta six months and had spent the majority of his time prior to that time devoted to Uncle Sam, Payne imagined that there was most likely a military connection. As part of an elite Ranger team—Project Chameleon—he, Danny, Guy and Jamie had enjoyed a certain…status amid their peers. It was quite possible that she recognized him and thought it would be a perverse ego deflator to stick him with the Bug.

Had he been anywhere but on his way to Gettysburg, he might have leaned toward that explanation. But considering the location and that niggling sense that Garrett hadn't leveled with him, Payne thought otherwise. Somehow the two so-called coincidences were related and fortunately, with a simple phone call, he felt like he could determine how.

Payne quickly checked in with the curbside rental help, then made his way to the Bug. Evidently having spotted him, the mystery woman immediately started the Hummer and competently angled it into traffic. Payne lost precious seconds trying to adjust the seat—he felt like a damned shark stuffed into a sardine can—but finally managed to jam it as far back as the track allowed and, shooting a look over his shoulder, smoothly fell in a few cars behind her. Fortunately the green Hummer was as conspicuous as his little car was. "Bet you hadn't counted on that, had you, you crafty she-devil?" Payne muttered. Of course, she probably hadn't counted on him following her either, but...

He consulted his directions and breathed a silent sigh of relief when she chose the same interstate exit that he needed to carry him toward the Bed and Breakfast Garrett had booked for him. Using the heavy traffic to his advantage, he zoomed up long enough to make out the tag number of her vehicle, then fell back a few paces, allowing himself to get momentarily hemmed in by a couple of eighteen wheelers.

Probably not the brightest move, Payne thought in retrospect as he fought to keep the little car from getting blown off the road, but he wasn't accustomed to driving something so damned...insubstantial. He thought longingly of his own SUV sitting in the Atlanta parking garage and determinedly snagged his cell phone from the clip at his waist. Time to put a name to the author of his recent misery, Payne decided.

Guy answered his direct line on the second ring. "McCann."

"It's me," Payne told him. "I need you to run a plate for me."

"Sure. What's up?"

Payne gave him the abbreviated version, glossing over the galling "driving-a-Bug" bit, hoping that Guy wouldn't notice. If he did, he'd roast him without mercy. "She's in a rental. Run a complete background check. I want to know what's going on here." That was probably his biggest understatement to date, he thought, annoyed at how thoroughly tied up a petty prank had gotten him.

"You think she's the 'something' Garrett was hiding from you?" Guy asked, predictably following his line of thinking.

Payne carefully negotiated traffic, noted once again that she'd taken the same route he was supposed to follow to the B&B. Another niggling suspicion began to form. He frowned. "I think there are one too many coincidences happening here," he said grimly.

"I'll take care of it and get back with you ASAP."

"Thanks, I appreciate it."

Guy laughed. "You ought to appreciate me not ragging you about *your* rental car. Hell, I'd give up a nut for a picture of that."

Payne fought a smile. "You'd have to sacrifice both nuts and your drill bit, partner. Trust me, it's not worth it."

Still laughing under his breath, Guy disconnected.

Traffic thinned along route fifteen, leaving Payne with no other choice but to fall in behind his pretty enigma. She could hardly fail to notice him there and he had to wonder if she was beginning to get a little spooked. Though he couldn't tell for certain—he was too low and she was too tall—he thought he saw her check her rearview mirror.

Five minutes later, she turned off Emmitsburg Road—which went through the center of historic Pickett's Charge—onto a long, winding driveway which led to The Dove's Nest Bed and Breakfast. Situated less than five miles from Gettysburg proper, the old B&B was a perfect place for history-loving tourists…or greedy Civil War buffs searching for the next coup to augment their collection, Payne silently added as he pulled the Bug right up next to her in the designated parking area.

With a galling amount of effort, he got out of the car, leaned an arm against the door, and peered at her from across the roof.

Looking distinctly uneasy, she climbed out of the Hummer and shot him what could only be described as a sick glance.

"Imagine that," he said, smiling wolfishly at her. "We're staying at the same place."

She managed a weak smile. "What were the odds?"

Exactly, Payne thought.

EMMA HAD BEEN a trifle nervous when she'd watched Brian Payne walk briskly to his rental car—he'd been in too much of a hurry for her comfort. With each step that she'd taken toward the Hummer, the more she'd realized that she'd made a serious tactical error.

Yes, seeing him crammed into that little car was gratifyingly hilarious, but in the end, the petty act had only served to put that legendary brain of his into suspicious-mode. Even from a safe distance in the Hummer she'd felt it.

Then, as she'd lessened the distance between herself and The Dove's Nest—the lovely B&B she'd gone online and chosen as her home base for the next several days—and he'd kept tailing her, a horrible thought had struck and had only been confirmed when she was less than five miles from

her ultimate destination. On a whim, Emma had
called ahead to The Dove's Nest and had asked to
be connected with Brian Payne's room. She'd
been told that he hadn't checked in yet and asked
would she like to leave a message for him upon
his arrival.

Er…that was a big fat negative.

At that point, the prudent thing to have done
would have undoubtedly been to find a different
place to stay. Unfortunately, "prudent" had never
been one of her strong points and she'd become
quite enamored with the thought of staying at the
old B&B. She'd even selected her room from the
beautiful photographs on the Web site. It was a
rare indulgence—one made doubly wonderful by
the fact that Hastings was picking up the tab—and
she hadn't wanted to change her plans merely to
accommodate Brian Payne.

Furthermore, it smacked of cowardice and
therefore went completely against her nature.

Clearly her one advantage was going to come
to a swift premature end, but that only meant that
she'd have to step up her game. She could do it,
Emma knew. Payne might be legendary but she
needed it more. Or at least that's what she planned
to tell herself because she had every intention of

beating him to the pocketwatch, collecting the final ten grand from Colonel Hastings and getting on with the rest of her life.

Since leaving the army, Emma had been so focused on helping her mother that she hadn't had the time to properly think about what it was she'd ultimately like to do with her life. She'd been too busy making ends meet to come up with a career plan, to nurse a dream. But Hastings's timely arrival had awakened an old ambition last night, one she hadn't thought about in years. Now, though, it had been dusted off and polished and it suddenly shone like the hope of a brand-new toy.

Vet school.

That's what she wanted to do. She'd always had a strong affinity for animals, generally related to animals of the four-legged variety better than to those who walked on two. Though her father had never had any special training, he'd always had a special bond with animals as well. She supposed she inherited the knack from him. She and her mother had lost him in a farming accident when she'd been eleven, a loss that still haunted her today.

Despite being an attractive woman with brains and wit, Lena had never remarried. John Edward

Langston had been *the* love of her life and when she lost him that had simply been it for her. Though Emma knew her mother had to get lonely from time to time, and had even gently suggested that her mother date, Lena had always given her a sad little smile and said, "My heart's just not in it, honey."

Because it was buried on Beacon Hill with her daddy, Emma thought now. Did she think that her father would want her mother to be lonely? No. But *wow* to be loved so thoroughly that the need to look for a replacement was simply out of the question. She remembered her parents, remembered how happy they'd been together, and a wistful tug pulled at her heart. When the time came, that's what she wanted. She wanted to be *thoroughly* loved.

Emma's lips twisted. Of course, so far all she'd managed to be was *partially* loved. Other than one relatively serious relationship when she'd first joined the military, she had little experience with love. Unfortunately finding a guy who wasn't intimidated by her drive had been a lot tougher than she'd have imagined. It wasn't something she thought she'd encounter in the army, but in the end she supposed boys were going to be boys no matter what the situation.

The first time she'd outperformed David, that had been the end of their relationship. Though they'd been together more than a year and he'd been her first, he hadn't even given her the courtesy of a face-to-face breakup—the little weasel had sent her a text message.

An army of one, my ass, Emma thought now. The coward.

Her gaze inexplicably slid to Payne, who was grabbing his gear from the back seat of the Bug. He wouldn't be a coward, she thought, feeling another rush of sexual attraction skip up her spine. Her lips twisted in a wry smile. Of course, by all accounts he was the most emotionally unavailable man on the planet, so he didn't have to be a coward, did he? He didn't invest anything and made it clear that he wasn't going to. Though it seemed a little cold to Emma, at least he was forthright. That was admirable, at any rate.

Furthermore, given the way her nipples tingled and her thighs melted every time he shot one of those cool blue looks at her, she could honestly imagine lust trumping common sense in favor of a night spent in his bed.

And coming from her that was saying something.

While she enjoyed good sex just as much as the next person, she'd always been too busy and too selective to have what one would call an active sex life. In fact, for the past year and some odd months, she hadn't had a sex life at all. David, quite honestly, had left a bad taste in her mouth and, other than the requisite ricochet lay with a guy who'd been a good friend—compliments of several self-pity cocktails of Jose Quervo—she'd been celibate.

In short, Emma was exceedingly picky about who she shared her body with and, while she had no romantic illusions about being passionately in love first, she had too much self-respect to simply open up shop for any old customer. Unlike a lot of her modern counterparts, she wasn't a convenience store, but preferred to think of herself an upscale boutique that only catered to worthy patrons. The idea drew a small smile.

"Do you need some help?" Payne asked her, stopping in front of the Hummer.

Still a gentleman, even after she'd made him rent that little car. That was sexy, too. Emma shook her head. "No, thanks. I've only got one bag."

"Only one? How long are you staying?"

It was an off-hand natural question and yet she knew he was fishing. "That depends," she said evasively. She grabbed her own bag, her purse and her laptop, then closed the door and locked up the Hummer.

"Depends on what?"

"How long it takes me to see everything I want to see," she said, not altogether lying. She wanted to see a pocketwatch before she left.

He inclined his head and waited on her to join him at the front of the vehicle, presumably so they could walk in together. She had an eerie feeling this was a portent of things to come. Hell, he'd practically dogged her every step since the airport. Shaking him wasn't going to be an easy task, particularly when her body was staging a rebellion against her— it was more inclined to shake…on top of him.

"What about you?" Emma decided to ask, hoping to derail her current line of thought. "How long are you in town?"

They rounded the side of the house, making their way to the front gate, which he obligingly held open for her. "A week, tops," he said.

Oh, goody, Emma thought. A week of torture. Sweet Lord, she had to find that damned pocket-watch first. "Is this your first trip to Gettysburg?"

He nodded. "What about you? First trip, also?"

"It is."

He smiled and shot her a humorous look which made the hair on her upper arms stand on end. "Amazing how much we have in common, isn't it?"

You have no idea, Emma thought, but managed a simple smile rather than retort. Then again, he probably did. That's why he'd latched onto her and had no intention of letting go until he found out all of her secrets. Then who knows what would happen?

One of two scenarios, she imagined. He'd either pack up his toys and move to another sandbox in order to keep her in the dark about his own progress in finding the pocketwatch. Or he'd adhere to the old keep-your-friends-close-and-your-enemies-closer adage and insist on playing with her so that he could keep tabs on her.

Perversely—because she was a horny moron, she supposed—she sincerely hoped it was the latter.

Emma huddled further into her jacket as they climbed the front steps to the old stone farmhouse. A historical plaque next to the door said Circa 1808 and the bright afternoon sun illuminated the various copper pots of pansies and other blooming winter flowers situated around the roomy porch.

Before Payne could grab the doorknob, a short, plump older woman wearing a quilted multicolored brocade pantsuit, a wild hat sporting peacock feathers and lots of gaudy jewelry barreled out, preceded by an enormous potbellied pig, who'd been dressed in a matching outfit, right down to the hat and pearls.

A startled laugh escaped Emma before she could check it.

"Mind your manners, Matilda, you ornery old hog," the woman chided. "Don't run over them." She looked at Emma and Payne. "Sorry about that," she said. "Tilda thinks she owns whatever path she's on. I'm Judith, by the way. My sister and her husband own The Dove's Nest, so Tilda and I are frequent visitors. I also conduct the ghost stories on Friday evenings. Hope to see you there," she said, then stumbled forward and grunted as her pig lunged once more for the steps. "Bye," she called hurriedly over her shoulder.

Emma and Payne stared dumbly at each other for a full five seconds before they both burst into laughter.

"Ghost stories?" Payne finally said, casting a glance at the house.

Emma nodded. "There are reportedly two

resident ghosts residing at The Dove's Nest. It's all on their Web site. What?" she asked at his skeptical glance. "Don't you believe in ghosts?"

"I've never met one."

Emma grinned. "Who knows? Maybe you'll get lucky."

She knew the instant the words left her mouth that it'd been the wrong thing to say, that her definition of "lucky" and his held two completely different meanings.

Wry humor sparked like a hot blue flame in those wintry eyes and the smallest hint of a sexy smile caught the corner of his supremely carnal lips, making her belly alternately knot and whirl. "Maybe I will."

And with that enigmatic, loaded comment he opened the door for her, ushering her inside.

The question was…to what? Her doom or desire?

With her luck, *probably both.*

5

BEGINNING TO FEEL more like a spider and less like a fly in this recent farce, Payne followed Hummer Girl—her name until he learned her proper one—into the foyer of The Dove's Nest B&B. For whatever reason, he'd imagined that Garrett had booked him into a Victorian-era bed and breakfast with chairs with spindly legs and lots of floral wallpaper. He'd imagined feeling like the proverbial bull in the china shop and staying hungry from lack of anything to eat beside little, bite-size sandwiches and hot tea.

The Dove's Nest was an old farmhouse with tall ceilings, hardwood floors—which had been blanketed with colorful rugs—and huge fireplaces which had done more than warm the backside of their genteel inhabitants. It was big and cozy and, while lushly appointed with substantial antiques, Payne didn't feel like there was a chair that wouldn't hold his weight. There were patrons in the dining room to the left and he caught the tantalizing whiff of prime rib and roasted potatoes.

He instantly revised his opinion of B&Bs and dubbed The Dove's Nest to his liking.

"Good afternoon," a petite older blonde greeted them as they neared the reception desk. "I'm Norah Gray. My husband Harry and I own The Dove's Nest." She jerked a finger toward the back of the house. "He's tooling around in the barn at the moment, but I'm sure he'll want to meet you two as soon as he comes back in." She smiled. "Do you have a reservation?"

"Yes," he and Hummer Girl said in unison.

Norah moved to the computer. "And whose name would it be under?"

Beside him, Hummer Girl blushed. "We're not together," she blurted out.

Norah blinked, then laughed softly at her gaffe. "I'm sorry. You came in together. I just assumed… Well," she said briskly. "Who would like to go first, then?"

"Ladies first," Payne said quickly and gave his reluctant companion a gentle nudge forward.

She turned and glared at him. And he knew why. She'd had her ID at the ready when they'd been standing in front of the car rental counter, but she hadn't had time to pull that trick here. No, now she was going to have to give up a little information—which he'd have figured out soon enough anyway, but… This way was better, Payne decided. Let her stew and steam and worry. Let her be bloody uncomfortable for a while. Like he'd been in that damned car.

"Okay, then," Norah said, turning her expectant gaze upon Hummer Girl.

"Emma Langsford," she said, evidently trying to ignore him out of existence.

Emma, Payne thought. It was an old-fashioned name, but it still seemed to fit.

"Ah," Norah said, smiling. "Here you are. I see you used our online reservation system and chose the Robert E. Lee room."

Payne felt a smile slide across his lips. He'd known her presence had something to do with Garrett, so while her room choice hadn't confirmed the connection in his mind…he did find it *particularly* interesting.

"Aw," he sighed, feigning disappointment. "I'd wanted that room."

Norah brightened. "How about I put you in the one next door? It's very similar."

"I didn't think you'd looked at the Web site," Emma said through a brittle smile.

"Oh, I haven't."

"Then how could you want what you haven't seen?"

"I'm a big fan of Robert E. Lee," he said, shrugging lightly. "Naturally, I'd want the room which bore his name."

She looked as though she'd like nothing better than to argue with him, but of course if she did that, she'd be tipping her hand. He didn't know precisely what sort of hand she held at the moment, but he enjoyed watching her guard the hell out of it all the same.

"Oh, I see you're from Mississippi," Norah enthused. "I've got family down in the Delta. Where is Marble Springs exactly?" she asked conversationally. Garrett's comment about B&B owners being a better source of information was proving to be quite true at the moment.

A *name* and a *hometown*, Payne thought, secretly enjoying Emma's increasing discomfort. *Come on, Norah*, he thought. *If you'd just cough up an address I could save Guy a lot of time.*

Emma's elfin face had turned a distinctly lovely shade of pink. "It's near Jackson," she said.

"Oh," Norah said. "Well, I'm sure it's a beautiful town. With a name like Marble Springs, it'd have to be, wouldn't it?" She handed Emma her key, along with a packet of information and free tickets to several of the local area attractions. "Let me know if you need anything at all, dear. We pride ourselves on our helpful service here at The Dove's Nest."

As well they should, Payne thought. She'd been pretty damned helpful to him already and he hadn't even gotten into his room yet.

She turned to Payne. "Now, let's see about getting you checked in, as well. Your name please?"

"Brian Payne."

Norah frowned. "Payne, Payne," she repeated thoughtfully, as though trying to remember something. "Oh! You had a call a few minutes ago."

From the corner of his eye he watched Emma scurry toward the staircase.

"A call?"

"Yes," Norah told him. "She didn't leave her name, just said she'd call back."

She? There wasn't a "she" who knew his whereabouts, Payne thought as he watched Emma Langsford's feet disappear up the stairs. He wasn't

entangled with any female who'd need posses-
sion of that information.

Furthermore, Ranger Security didn't have any
women on payroll—even their secretary was a
man, a multitasking, sticky-noting, filing guru of
unknown sexual orientation. Not that it mattered.
So long as Juan-Carlos did the job and didn't hit
on him, Payne didn't care whose team he batted for.

The only person who might have called him—
and this was a huge stretch—was Jamie's wife,
Audrey. But that seemed unlikely as well because
she had his cell number. Anyone who needed to
get in touch with him immediately knew to catch
him on the cell. He kept it on and with him at all
times, even at home in his loft.

"Would you like the room next to Ms. Langsford, then?" Norah asked, interrupting his
thoughts. "Like I said, it's very similar to the
Robert E. Lee room."

Payne's gaze darted to the ceiling where he
could imagine he saw Emma hurrying down the
hall and he sighed and shook his head at his own
thickness.

Sonofabitch.

It had been *her.*

She'd called here.

That's why she hadn't been surprised that he'd continued to follow her. Just as he'd suspected, she *had* known who he was all along. By placing that call, she'd merely confirmed her own suspicions about where he was staying while in Gettysburg and her hasty retreat the instant Norah mentioned the missed call only increased her guilty behavior.

Payne didn't know which he was more—irritated or impressed.

Or turned on.

Odd that he should find her duplicitous crafty behavior so damned sexually provoking, but he couldn't deny the blood hurtling toward his balls or the insane urge he had to take the stairs two at a time, bang on her door until she opened it—and then bang *her.*

Until she forgot everyone's name but his. And she agreed to trade rental cars with him.

"Mr. Payne?" Norah questioned, her brow wrinkled in a line of concern.

"Oh, sorry," he said. "I was lost in my own thoughts." Lurid ones, he didn't add. "The room next to Ms. Langsford's will do nicely, thank you."

Norah efficiently checked him into his room, provided him with a key and coupons—the same as she had Emma—then wished him a pleasant stay. "Please let us know if there's anything at all that you need," she said. "There are books, movies, magazines and a couple of cable internet connections for our guests' use in the library."

"Excellent, thank you," Payne told her. So the house might be circa 1808, but thankfully it supported new millennium technology. He shot her a smile, then made his way up the wide staircase.

She'd put him in the Potomac Suite and, as promised, the Robert E. Lee room was just next door. She was in there now, Payne thought as he inserted his key into the lock. She was in there, plotting and planning and trying to coordinate her next move. Clearly she had an agenda and the sooner he found out what it was, the better off he'd be.

Payne's first thought was to place a call to Garrett and demand further details regarding this so-called mission, but rather than do that, he decided to check in with Guy first. Granted, going to his former commanding officer held considerable appeal, but going to him armed with every bit of information he could get his hands on first appealed even more.

He made a cursory inspection of the room— made sure the linens were fresh, the bathroom clean and the bed to his liking—then sat down in a comfortable chair next to the window and dialed Guy once more.

"Emma Langsford," Payne told him without preamble.

"I know," Guy told him. "I've been on the phone with her mother."

Payne sat forward. "Her mother?"

"Lucky for you she's chatty," Guy told him. "I called, pretending that I was an old friend from her military days and she—"

"Military days?"

"She did eight years, but didn't re-up. She was needed at home. Her grandfather was dying."

Granted he didn't know her, but he could definitely see where that would fit into her character. "Go on."

"You're not going to like this," he warned.

"I wasn't expecting to."

"According to her mother, she's on a 'mission' for Colonel Hastings."

"She told you that?"

"No, she told me that she was taking care of some business for her old boss. I did some quick digging and filled in Hastings's name."

"So what business is she doing?" He had a grim suspicion, of course, but wanted confirmation.

"The same business you are. Evidently Garrett and Hastings are both after the watch and they're in the habit of placing bets. Garrett has pitted you against Hastings's girl. Without telling you about it."

That manipulative old bastard, Payne thought, as a red haze suddenly swam before his gaze. He'd bartered his freedom for a damned bet between friends? He knew why he was doing it—he was repaying a debt. But what was Emma's angle?

After a moment he decided to ask. "What's her motive? Do you know?"

Guy hesitated. "I don't know, but I have a suspicion."

"And?"

"The oldest motivator—money."

"Hastings is paying her?" Payne asked. Geez God, did everything have to come back to cash? "Did her mother tell you that?"

"No, but I got the impression that things were pretty tight. Emma's put off going to college, but her mother was quick to tell me that vet school was in order as soon as she got back. She was quite proud, went on and on about what a fabulous girl her Emma was."

So the woman was selling her daughter, Payne

thought. Which meant there was no significant other lurking in Emma Langston's past, otherwise her mother wouldn't have gone to the trouble of singing her praises. His spirits lifted marginally.

"Surely to God he's not paying her enough to put her through vet school," Payne said, unwilling to believe that the damned watch could be worth that kind of money.

"Hastings has definitely got it, but no I don't think he's giving her that much either. It's probably enough to get her started, though, which would be a powerful motivator."

Yeah. Enough to water her dream.

Shit.

"There's more," Guy said.

Another blistering curse singed the telephone line between then. "What?"

"If the rumors surrounding her character are true, then the reason Hastings chose her is because she's a tad on the ruthless side."

Payne didn't know if he'd peg her as ruthless—for whatever reason that didn't seem to fit—but from what he'd seen so far she was definitely crafty. Between the Hummer incident and her phone call to The Dove's Nest, she'd shown that she was quick and sharp-minded, at the very least.

"What are you going to do?" Guy asked.

Payne pushed a hand through his short hair. "I don't know."

"If I were you, I'd call Garrett and tell him to kiss my ass, then I'd get on the first flight back to Atlanta."

"I can't do that," Payne said. "I gave my word."

"And he's abused it," Guy retorted. "Honor is one thing, Payne. Being used is another."

When it came right down to it, an order was still an order and Payne's word was still his word. But there was no point in trying to explain the difference to Guy. Even in the military he'd lived by his own terms. He'd just been so good that the powers that be never cared.

"I'll call you when I figure out my game plan," Payne said. "Thanks for checking into this for me."

"Watch your back, man," Guy said. "Sounds like this chick is capable of putting a knife in it. Call me if you need anything else."

Payne disconnected, scanned the room for a liquor cabinet and sighed when he realized that there wasn't one. What he needed right now was a stiff shot of whiskey and a new game plan, because Garrett's bet-of-omission had certainly thrown a monkey wrench into his plans.

After all, he'd planned to come to Gettysburg, swiftly locate the pocketwatch—if it even existed, which still remained to be seen—turn the damned thing over to Garrett and go home.

End of favor.

Honor intact.

Debt paid.

Now… Now securing the pocketwatch for Garrett's scheming benefit meant that he'd be robbing Emma Langsford—ruthless or not—of her brand-new beginning and her start-up money for vet school. Either way the scenario went down, he was going to wind up the villain.

Whether it was Garrett's or Emma's remained to be seen.

DESPITE THE DARK CLOUD she could hear moving into the room next door, Emma still loved her room and didn't regret the B&B choice. The interior had been outfitted with a general in mind and as such had all the amenities. A huge four-poster bed hung with lacy curtains was centered on one wall, the matching antique pieces situated to perfection.

She had a lovely sitting area, complete with a tea service in front of a window which overlooked the grounds. No doubt it was nicer in the spring when a blanket of green grass and flowers bloomed over the meadow, but something about the stark beauty of the landscape below was equally appealing to her. She had a good view of the barn, of a man she imagined to be her host, Harry, and a pair of beautiful horses—one a strawberry roan and the other a dappled gray—who were munching lazily on a bale of hay.

She'd inspected the bathroom, delighted over the big claw-foot tub—it was very similar to the one at home—and couldn't wait to fill it up with hot water and the scented bubble bath which had been left on the counter. A small plate of oatmeal-raisin cookies and a cool glass of lemonade had arrived at her door within minutes of her checking into her room and Emma currently sat curled up in a comfortable chair by the window, momentarily enjoying the view, the tasty cookies and a chance to simply unwind without being caught in Brian Payne's crosshairs.

He was next door, so she knew the sensation would be short-lived. Furthermore, after the way he'd nudged her forward and insisted that she check in first, she'd had no other choice but to give Norah her name…which meant that he had it now, as well. Therefore, it was only a matter of time before he put that considerable brain-power toward finding out what she was doing here.

Lying wouldn't be an option, not that she'd ever been all that good at it anyway. She had a hard enough time remembering the truth, much less the ability to keep track of lies. Not to mention, it just simply made her uncomfortable. She liked knowing the truth and couldn't very well insist on it if she was going to be any less honest, right?

Emma chased a bite of cookie with a sip of lemonade and resigned herself to the coming week of sheer hell. Once Payne found out what she was after, he'd step up his game and she'd be forced to outpace him or lose, which was out of the question. She needed this too badly to let him take it from her. She had no idea what he'd done with himself when he'd left the military—he and his friends had left after the death of one of their own—but from what little she'd heard, he wasn't hurting for money.

Technically that was none of her business and shouldn't be a factor, but whatever he had riding on this couldn't mean as much to him as it did to her. He'd been a pawn in a bet and, while she'd never dealt with Colonel Garrett, she didn't think he was backing Payne with the promise of cash the way that Hastings was backing her. She didn't have any idea what Payne was getting out of this, but when they cleared the air between them, she had every intention of finding out. It shouldn't matter—she had to look out for her own interests, after all—and yet it did.

At any rate, she'd already gone over the initial information Hastings had given her on the watch and planned to get started ASAP. She needed to put a call in to her mother, then mosey downstairs and start pumping Norah for information. Although she longed for a nap, she couldn't afford the luxury, not with Major Payne next door. The name drew a smile. No doubt he'd taken considerable ribbing in the military for a name like that.

Letting go a sigh, Emma reluctantly got up from her chair and snagged her cell phone from her purse. She hit one on speed dial and waited for her mother to answer.

"Lena's," came the familiar reply.

"Hi, Mom. Just wanted to let you know that I made it to the B&B. I left the number on the desk at home, but you'll have better luck catching me on my cell if you need to."

"Oh, honey, I was just about to call you," her mother said, sounding particularly excited.

"What's going on?"

"You had a call. From a guy," she added significantly.

And it would be significant because she hadn't had a guy call her in months. For whatever reason, Emma's belly twisted and ballooned with dread.

"Did he leave a name?"

"As a matter of fact, he did—Guy McCann. He said he was an old friend from your military days and he was trying to catch up with you. I hope you don't mind, dear, but he sounded like such a nice boy, I gave him your cell phone number," she said brightly. "Did he call?"

Guy McCann. One of Payne's equally notorious pals. Things had progressed a lot faster than she'd anticipated. Hell, he'd only had her name for ten minutes. Surely to God— "When did he call?" she asked as another suspicion took hold.

"An hour or so ago. You sound funny. Is something wrong?"

"No," Emma lied, unconvincingly as usual. How on earth had he gotten her name? She knew that the car rental clerk had never uttered it aloud and she'd been careful to keep her rental agreement out of Payne's line of sight. Her gaze swung to her bag—she hadn't tagged it. How the hell—

"Emma? What's—"

Oh, sweet Lord. If her mother had been charmed enough to give out her cell phone number, God only knows what else she'd told McCann. Another bubble of dread burst in her ever-sickening belly. "Mom, what else did you tell him? You didn't tell him why I'm in Gettysburg, did you?"

A telling, horrible pause, then, "Not in so many words. Why?"

Emma sank back into her chair and massaged the bridge of her nose. "What exactly did you tell him?"

"Just that you were working on something for your old boss," her mother said. "Have I done something wrong?"

"No, Mom," Emma told her. She'd just been her breezy, cheerful self, which was all smooth-talking Guy McCann had needed her to be.

"Who is he?" her mother asked, belatedly catching on to the fact that he wasn't a potential boyfriend after all.

Emma brought her mother up to speed. "If anyone else calls, play dumb, Mom." Not that it would matter now. The cat was out of the bag. He knew her name, he knew that she was working on something for her old boss. Then there'd been the Robert E. Lee room tip-off. Ugh. She was dead in the water. If Payne didn't know exactly what she was up to yet, he would before long.

"I'm sorry, Emma," her mother said, sounding genuinely sorry. "I just thought—"

"No worries, Mom. It's all right. It was inevitable, anyway."

"That was so *sneaky,*" her mother said, offended at last. "I've got a good mind to call him back and give him a piece of my mind. Of all the low-down, rotten—"

Emma chuckled, debating the merits of caller ID. "Mom, forget about it," she insisted. "It's fine."

After multiple assurances, Lena finally calmed down. "If you're sure, dear," she said, somewhat mollified.

"I'm sure. I've got to run. I'll check in with you later, okay?"

"Be careful."

"I will," Emma promised. She almost told Lena that she wasn't in any danger, but in another minute that might not be true. Because she was

about to go next door and level the playing field
with Brian Payne.

The whole time she'd been trying to calm her
mother down, Emma had begun to seethe. He'd had
his damned friend call her mother, for pity's sake.
What kind of sportsmanship was that? Was it her
fault that Garrett hadn't leveled with him? What?
Was *she* supposed to owe him some sort of courtesy?

Horse shit.

She didn't owe him a damned thing and nobody—*nobody*—even a badass former Ranger,
was allowed to mess with her mother.

Emma tossed her cell phone on the bed, then
marched out into the hall and abruptly rapped on
his door. Irritation straightened her spine and
vibrated every muscle in her body. He might have
earned the name Major Payne…but she was about
to teach him the meaning of the moniker.

6

PAYNE WAS IN THE PROCESS of putting his clothes away in the armoire when he heard Emma's door open. That was fast, he thought, muttering a curse. Either she was much more efficient at unpacking than he was, or she simply hadn't bothered. For whatever reason—probably stupidity—the knowledge drew a smile. Clearly she had her sights set firmly on the money—on her new beginning—and taking the time to unpack didn't warrant her attention.

He grimaced. Given what he'd just learned, it probably shouldn't warrant his either, but old habits died hard. He liked order. Everything had a place and Payne's world was a lot clearer when those things were as they should be. It irritated the hell out of him that he was going to have stop unpacking just to tail her, but it had to be done. Until he figured out how he intended to handle this, he had to keep her close at hand. He had to make sure that she didn't, by some miracle of chance, get the jump on him. Bested by a woman? Geez God, he'd never live it down.

He abandoned his shaving kit, grabbed his keys and started for the door. Someone knocked on it before he could grasp the knob. Now this was a surprise, Payne thought. Logic told him that it had to be her, but logic had also told him that she'd most likely avoid him like the plague.

He'd been wrong.

Little warning bells sounded in his head at the anomaly, but he scarcely had time to heed them before he opened the door.

Five feet of pissed-off female greeted him. "Where the hell do you get off having your friend call my mother?" she demanded, advancing angrily into his room.

Payne could pretend not to know what she was talking about, but decided that would be a waste of time. If she came here for a showdown, he'd give her one. "I didn't tell my friend to call your mother. I told him to find out who you were and what you were doing here." He shrugged, watched her interestedly scan his room. "He called your mother in the process."

She pivoted, cocked her head and her irritated

dark blue gaze found his. "Did it ever occur to you, Boy Genius, to simply ask?"

Boy Genius? "It occurred to me," he returned mildly. "It also occurred to me that you would lie. I distinctly recall asking you at the airport if we'd ever met and you said no."

"That wasn't a lie. We *haven't* ever met."

Payne crossed his arms over his chest and leaned against the bedpost. "But you knew who I was."

"You didn't ask me if I knew you—you asked if we'd ever met. The answer was no and *that* was not a lie."

He made a humming noise under his breath. "I understand your mother is a beautician—did you learn how to split hairs from her?"

She stiffened once more. "You and your friends had better leave my mother out of this. That was a shitty thing to do." Her lips twisted. "And here I'd heard you had a reputation for being honorable."

That dart found a mark. "And I've heard you have a reputation for being ruthless."

His found a mark as well, judging by the blinking pause that met his statement. "I don't give a damn what you've heard," she said, clearly lying. "I'm not ruthless, but I *am* determined and since I know you're here looking for the same thing that I am, it would be extremely stupid of me to tip you off, wouldn't it?" She snorted. "I don't owe you a damned thing, especially not an explanation."

All true, he knew, and yet he couldn't help being disappointed. "No more than I owe you anything. Given the circumstances, I find it highly ironic that you don't have any qualms about keeping me in the dark, but get pissed off when I use whatever means necessary to shed a little light on things. Guy shouldn't have called your mother, but am I sorry that he did? No."

"That was low."

"So was sticking me in that little car," he said, surprised at the level of irritation he heard in his own voice.

She smiled and flicked an imaginary speck of lint off her cuff. "No, that was a stroke of genius. How does it drive, by the way?"

"Better than I expected. You should really work on handling that Hummer better, though. You were all over the road."

A total lie, but he couldn't stand the smug look on her face. It was provoking, and Brian Payne never allowed himself to be provoked. It meant that he wasn't in control of his own emotions, and that this little slip of a female could incite him into exchanging juvenile barbs told him he was wading into uncharted waters.

Her eyes widened in outrage. "I was not all over the road—I *owned it*. There's a difference, but I guess you couldn't see that perched five inches off the pavement, could you?"

This was pointless, Payne decided. Time to move things into a more productive line of conversation. "How much is Hastings paying you?"

"That's none of your damned business. What's Garrett paying you?" she shot back.

"Garrett and I have different terms, but if you'll leave right now, I'll match Hastings's offer simply to get you to leave."

Payne blinked, certain those words hadn't just come out of his mouth. Surely to God he hadn't just tried to *bribe* this woman simply to be rid of her. He didn't bribe anyone. He didn't need to. He played by the rules and he won, fair and square. What the hell was wrong with him? He wasn't threatened by her, dammit, though given the suddenly crafty glint in her eye, that was the conclusion she'd instantly leaped to. A litany of anatomically impossible curses ricocheted through his head.

"That's a kind offer, Major Payne. Very gener-
ous," she said, with a patronizing little smile that
made his teeth grind together. "But I think I'll
stick with my original plan."

He leveled a cool stare at her, purposely letting
a beat slide into five before he responded. "You're
in over your head. Are you sure?"

She met his hard stare with a surprising amount
of lead in her own. "I made an agreement with
Colonel Hastings," Emma told him. "And, believe
it or not, my word is worth more than your
money."

Honorable and ruthless—now there was a combination one didn't encounter very often, Payne
thought, reluctantly impressed. Unfortunately, it
put them right back where they started.

At odds.

Payne nodded. "I am also a man of my word
and I've given it to Colonel Garrett, so may the
best man win."

Those ripe strawberry lips slid into another provoking smile. "No worries. The best *woman* will."

Plucky and sexy. A lethal combination. She
might not be the only one in over her head, he
thought, slightly alarmed.

"Tit-for-tat time," Emma said. "You know

Hastings has offered me a nice bonus in exchange for finding this pocketwatch. What's Garrett giving you?"

Freedom, Payne thought instantly.

The final payment on a life he desperately wanted to leave behind. This favor for Garrett was Payne's last tie to his military career, to Danny's death. Visiting Arlington again the day before yesterday had been like sticking a hot poker into a gaping wound.

Though Payne knew he wasn't directly responsible for Danny's death, he'd been the one who'd coordinated that mission—*his* tactics had failed—and, as a result, no matter what anybody ever told him, he bore a major share of the responsibility.

Naturally they'd all known the risks—they'd known that death had been a possibility—but up until the moment Jamie had carried Danny Levinson's lifeless body over that hill, it hadn't been real to them.

They'd been *invincible.*

Untouchable.

They'd never failed. Hell, they hadn't failed then, either—they'd just come back as three rather than four.

Did Payne doubt his mission? His service? The

belief in a greater good? No. Somebody had to do the hard work and he'd always prided himself on being one of those people—on having the stones to step up—on shouldering the burden that had been passed down from generations of fearless Americans who'd laid down their lives for the freedoms and wealth their nation enjoyed.

But something had changed the night Danny died—Guy and Jamie had felt it as well. It was as though the spark that had made them the unit they'd been had been snuffed out right along with their friend's life. Suddenly all that had mattered was getting out—passing the torch—and starting over.

Guy had been the first to bring it up. It had been after the funeral, but before they'd even left the cemetery. A sea of white crosses, the newest of which belonged to their friend, lay out before them. "I don't know about you guys," he'd said. "But this Bama boy is sick of fishing and ready to cut bait."

Both he and Jamie had been thinking the same thing. They'd merely nodded and, after a final goodbye, turned and walked away. Shortly afterward, they'd come up with the idea of Ranger Security and Payne had once again lost himself in the details.

Deadened his pain with daily minutiae.

One way or another, though, by the end of the week, his debt to Garrett would have been paid. God willing, he could make a clean break and, while he never expected to understand Danny's death—to an organized mind, there was no way to process senselessness—he hoped that he could come to terms with it. To move on and get past a margin of the guilt. For whatever reason, this favor to Garrett provided him with a way to do it. *That* was the chance Garrett was giving him.

That's why he couldn't bail.

But he couldn't tell her that any more than he could explain it to Guy, so he twisted his lips into a semblance of a smile and fired her line right back at her. "It's none of your damned business."

READING BRIAN PAYNE WAS like staring at a broken-down TV that occasionally flashed into focus. It was nearly impossible to make sense of the whole program with only a few frames for guidance. And that's how Emma felt now. From the instant she'd barged into this room, she'd been catching flashes of Payne, but never the total picture.

For instance, only a second ago she'd glimpsed a pain so stark that it made her breath catch. Then just as quickly it was gone, only to be replaced by a fleeting look of fierce determination. Finally he'd told her his reasons for looking for the pocketwatch were none of her damned business and was currently staring at her as though he wasn't quite sure what to do or say next.

Brian Payne at a loss. Surely this was a momentous occasion, she thought, suppressing a smile.

Emma was suddenly aware of his big shoulder leaned so casually against the bedpost, the intriguing landscape of muscle displayed beneath his khaki cable-knit sweater. He'd pushed the sleeves up a bit, revealing forearms that were equally muscled and covered with a smooth dusting of light blonde hair.

His hands were big and capable and a rush of heat flooded her belly as a picture of those hands splayed across her naked back leaped instantly to mind. He could easily span her waist, she realized, and the knowledge was like an immediate aphrodisiac, making her senses swim, her nipples tingle and her stomach flutter. He reminded her of a palomino stallion she'd seen once, huge and glorious and splendidly proportioned. Harnessed energy and strength, ready for action should the need arise.

A soft breath stuttered from between her lips as the rest of the room seemed to shrink and the bed loomed even larger into focus. In less than a blink of an eye, she imagined them naked and sweaty, her riding him until every bit of that legendary ice melted, leaving nothing but a sizzling, steamy puddle of satisfied man. Fire licked through her veins, flaring hotter in her breasts and settling in for a slow burn in her sex.

A knock at the door startled Emma out of her daydream. Payne pushed away from the bedpost and answered it, giving her a chance to wipe some of the imaginary dribble off her chin.

Good Lord, she had to get a grip. He was a man, Emma told herself. That was all.

Yeah, and the Great Wall of China was a chain link fence, too, she thought with an inward snort, briefly wondering if sexual attraction could make a person's reason completely snap. Hers had definitely suffered some sort of fracture over the past few hours, otherwise she wouldn't be standing in her competition's room, imagining carnal acts of depravity fit for a premium porn channel.

"Cookies and lemonade," Emma heard a familiar friendly voice say. It was the same older gentleman—Matthew, Norah's father, if memory served—who'd delivered her refreshments, as well.

Payne murmured his thanks, then went to give the man a tip.

"Oh, we'll have none of that," Matthew said with a soft chuckle. "Just compliment the cook and that's tip enough. Enjoy your stay."

Payne looked momentarily out of his element, as though he wasn't accustomed to anyone refusing a tip. Given the trendy clothes, the designer watch she'd noticed only moments ago and the pricey Italian loafers on his enormous feet, she imagined he was more accustomed to staying at a five-star hotel than a quaint B&B.

Emma paused, giving him the once over again, this time for completely different reasons than she'd had only moments before. *Well, I'll be damned,* she thought with belated realization.

She'd missed it—*money*.

Evidently she'd been too bowled over by his seemingly infinite sex appeal to note it before. She'd been too busy imagining him naked to pay any attention to what he'd been wearing, but now that she took a closer look…it was obvious.

Hell, the watch and the shoes alone would pay

for a new car she wanted, Emma realized. She considered him thoughtfully. Either Brian Payne was relatively wealthy, or he was in serious debt and, for whatever reason, the latter didn't fit. He didn't seem like the extravagant type.

Furthermore, this answered another question. Whatever his reasons, she could safely assume that he wasn't here for the money. She seriously doubted Garrett could pay him enough.

So if it wasn't cash, then what was his motivator? Had Garrett offered him something else? Did he owe Garrett? And if so, then what? She couldn't imagine—

"Cookie?" Payne offered before she could ponder the conundrum any further.

"No, thanks," Emma told him. "I've already had some."

"Right," Payne said with a knowing quirk of his lips. "You were quicker about getting up here than I was. You practically sprinted up the stairs."

Emma tucked her hair behind her ear. "I needed to stretch my legs."

He selected a cookie. "You needed to get away from me."

She winced, making light of the too true

comment. "We have spent a lot of time together recently."

"Then you aren't going to like the next few days."

Oh, hell. "What do you mean by that?" she asked cautiously.

He lifted his shoulders in a negligent shrug. "I'm in the room next door, we're both looking for the pocketwatch. We're bound to run into each other. Coincidentally, of course," he added, his lethally sexy lips sliding into a smile that held more warning than humor.

It was just as she suspected. He'd pegged her as the enemy and intended to keep her close. A perverse thrill swept through her, even as a tense ball of dread landed in her stomach. She let go a somewhat shaky breath.

Game on, then, Emma thought.

"You could always move to another hotel," she suggested, just to annoy him.

Payne actually laughed. "Now what would be the fun in that?"

"I didn't realize we were here to have fun," she said.

In fact, she had too much riding on this to label it fun. But given what she knew about Payne and considering Hastings's you-don't-have-to-play-by-the-rules comment, she could sure as hell make it interesting for him. If he thought she was simply going to allow him to follow her around without putting up any resistance, then he'd better use that big brain of his to think again, Emma thought. She had too much riding on this to allow him to toy with her.

"Odd how Garrett didn't tell you about me," she commented, shooting him a speculative glance.

His expression turned grim. "'Odd' isn't how I'd describe it," he said, his voice an ominous mixture of anger and promised retribution.

"Oh? Then how *would* you describe it?" Blatant fishing, but she had nothing more to lose at this point, right?

"Stupid."

Oy. Emma waited, hoping he would elaborate. After a moment, when it became annoyingly obvious that he wasn't going to, she decided to do a little more excavating. Or blasting, because she could see that trying to get anything out of this guy would be like trying to coax water from a stone. "Why do you think he decided to omit that information?"

That cool blue gaze met hers over the rim of his

lemonade glass. He took a swallow, seeming to be weighing the merit of sharing his opinion with her. "I imagine because he knew it would piss me off. I'm not used to having my services bartered in a bet. It's insulting."

She had to agree with him on that. Initially she'd been too excited over the money to really stop and think about how Garrett and Hastings had pitted them against each other like lab rats, eagerly watching from a distance to see whose gopher would win. Unfortunately, right, wrong or indifferent, she didn't have the luxury of dwelling on the insult. She had to keep her eyes on the prize, so to speak, and couldn't afford to consider Hastings's offer as anything more than a business arrangement.

Another thought struck. "You said you'd had Guy McCann find out who I was and what I was doing here? How did he do that without my name?" That was something that had been really bugging her. She'd been too careful about not revealing her identity.

"I had him call the rental car company."

"And they gave him my name? Isn't that against the law?"

Payne shrugged. "The clerk was young. It's amazing what kind of information people will share over the phone, particularly when you tell them you're with a security company."

Emma grimaced. Her mother included. "Security company?"

"Me, Guy McCann and Jamie Flanagan started our own business when we left the military—Ranger Security. We're based in Atlanta."

"Congratulations," Emma said, because it was the appropriate response.

Meanwhile the cookies she'd eaten a few moments ago were whirling around her gut like a load of laundry on the spin cycle and were undoubtedly going to make an encore appearance if she didn't get a grip. He'd started a security business? she thought faintly. He'd become a friggin' private investigator? Hell, he had resources at his disposal that were more than likely going to make this a walk in the park for him.

Surely Hastings had known this, Emma thought, feeling blindsided by the news. And, for reasons known only to himself, he'd chosen not to tell her. No doubt this was akin to the unhappy sensation Payne had felt upon learning of Garrett's duplicity, she decided, and suddenly felt a smidge of belated regret for his situation.

Nevertheless, Payne had most likely researched

the pocketwatch and was operating on more information than the few facts Hastings had passed along to her. In addition, Payne had a staff in Atlanta who could handle a lot of the menial things—phone calls, etc.—that she'd have to take care of herself. Her gaze slid to Payne and an unhappy truth surfaced—one that, in light of this new information, she could not deny.

If she wanted this—and she did, so *very, very desperately*—then she didn't have any choice but to be ruthless.

And she instinctively knew he was the type of person who would hate her for it.

7

SHE'D GIVEN HIM THE SLIP.

Payne was so astounded he could hardly believe it. Years of special training in one of the most elite armies in the world, hours logged in reconnaissance missions which would have made men of lesser mental fiber crack, not to mention the fact that he was The Specialist, dammit, a nickname he'd earned for being so bloody good at everything.

And yet one little woman had somehow managed to not only exit her room—hell, he'd been listening for that—but had somehow managed to crank up a friggin' Hummer and drive it out of the parking lot without him hearing it.

If he wasn't so damned annoyed, he'd be impressed.

As it was, he was *pissed*. His face burned from what he grimly suspected was the first blush he'd had since puberty and he silently thanked his lucky stars that neither Guy nor Jamie were here to witness his humiliation.

To make matters worse, breakfast smelled out of this world—the tantalizing scent of French toast, eggs, bacon and sausage permeated the air—but would he get to enjoy any of it? No, he thought as his stomach rumbled with hunger. Because, thanks to little Ms. Competitive, he didn't have time. He was not accustomed to being thwarted or missing breakfast and as such, had gruesome predictions as to how the rest of his day would go.

"Good morning, Mr. Payne," Norah called cheerfully as he descended the stairs. "Did you sleep well?"

"Yes," he lied, with an automatic smile. Actually, he'd barely slept at all—he'd been too busy keeping tabs on Emma to get a decent night's sleep. Frankly, he hadn't expected her to get started so early. He'd heard her rattling around in her room until the wee hours of the morning and had been secretly relieved when she'd finally— seemingly—settled. He scowled.

Clearly that had been a ruse.

"My father has laid quite a spread for breakfast this morning," she told him. "Will you be joining us?"

"Your father?"

"I'm sure you met him yesterday," Norah said. "He was the one who delivered the refreshments to your room after you checked in." She smiled fondly, as though sharing a secret. "He's meticulous about that. *'Friendly service and feed 'em,'* that's what he always says."

Just compliment the cook, Payne remembered him saying. He just hadn't imagined that the older gentleman *was* the cook. No doubt that little tidbit had been on the Web site, as well, he thought, irritated with himself for not researching things more thoroughly.

Furthermore, he'd also been surprised—and thrown off guard—when his tip had been refused. Frankly, he was used to his money talking—good service equaled a good gratuity. Bad service, bad tip. It was a simple enough system.

Worse, he was quite certain, given the speculative look Emma had given him once he'd closed the door, that she'd witnessed his fleeting misstep. No doubt she'd read some sort of emotional imbalance or some other such nonsense into his reaction as a result. Women were like that, he knew. Constantly speculating, digging and leaping to the conclusions about men—generally the wrong ones.

He was being surly and uncharitable, he knew, but he couldn't seem to help himself. Something about her and this entire situation had gotten under his skin, and between the flash-fire attraction, Garrett's lie of omission and his limited choices when it came to whether to honor his word or let Emma Langsford have her brand-new start, he wasn't what one could call *chipper.* He felt his expression blacken to match his mood. Actually, he'd never been chipper, but that was beside the point.

He passed on the breakfast and was almost out the door when a thought struck. "Norah, you haven't seen Ms. Langsford this morning, have you?"

"Oh, yes," she said. "She was out bright and early. She said she wanted to do some driving before she hit the local antique shops. She's a lovely girl, isn't she?"

Antique shops—his first plan of attack, as well. Dealers were typically a fount of information, particularly if a person was looking for a specific piece. Furthermore, dealers trolled the estate sales for treasured articles, and the chances of the pocketwatch winding up on sale in one of the local shops was a far more promising scenario than if it ended up with a private collector.

"You know," Norah said with a speculative gleam and a cautious smile, "we like to pair our guests up for dinner. Would you be interested in dining with Ms. Langsford during your stay?" He could practically see the matchmaking wheels turning in her romantic mind.

Ah, Payne thought. His first turn of good luck. "Could you do that?" he asked, playing along, delighted, but not for the reasons she suspected.

She beamed at him. "Certainly."

"Excellent," Payne told her. "That'll give me something to look forward to tonight."

And it would. If by some chance he didn't manage to find her today, then at least he'd be able to pin her down this evening and find out exactly how she'd managed to slip under his radar this morning.

Payne opened the front door and stepped out into the cold, bracing air. His breath fogged in front of his face and frost crunched beneath his feet as he made his way down the front porch steps. The Bug looked like an iced-over glittering insect in the bright morning sun. Despite the cold, the sky was more blue than gray, promising warmer temperatures later in the day.

Dreading the moment he would have to contort himself to get into the car, he fished the keys from his front pocket and hit the remote to unlock the doors. Grumbling under his breath—at least until he caught himself—he wedged his body into the car, turned on the ignition and waited for the engine to warm up before putting it into reverse.

The instant he lifted his foot off the clutch and felt the car lurch backward, he knew something was wrong.

Loud banging was never a good sound.

Summoning patience from a hidden, untapped source, he put the Bug back in to neutral, set the parking brake and climbed back out of the car. A quick trip to the rear of the vehicle revealed the problem.

"*Determined,* my ass," Payne said, glaring at the flattened tires.

She *was* ruthless.

A muscle jumped in his jaw and his back teeth ground together until he felt certain the enamel would crack. It was well done, he'd give her that. If she'd sabotaged the front tires, he would have noticed instantly. Instead, she'd banked on him being too preoccupied with the idea that she'd beaten him out of the gate and, as such, she'd let the air out of both rear tires. And he could just imagine her gleeful, gorgeous face while she did it, too, the she-devil, Payne thought.

He was suddenly hit with the idiotic, immature urge to kick the car, a lamentable lack of control he would ordinarily never entertain. Only by sheer force of will did he manage to get his temper under control.

He stood stock-still, counted to ten, then to twenty and then he imagined the next best thing to being able to throttle her at the moment—and that was putting her firmly on her back. He'd never been into bondage, but found the idea of tying her spread-eagle to the bed posts in his room upstairs distinctly arousing.

Naked limbs, silken skin, pouty nipples and a thatch of dark curls between creamy, inviting thighs...

If it wouldn't be such a crime to cover up that beautiful, sexy mouth of hers, he'd think about securing it with duct tape and then taking her six ways to Sunday. Until every ruthless, under-handed, vengeful impulse was wrung from her perfect little body.

He'd watched her yesterday, knew that she was every bit as tied up in this unholy attraction as he was. He'd had the privilege of watching those sugared-violet eyes turning a midnight blue, had watched her pupils dilate with need. She'd absently licked her lips, a silent, unspoken invitation, and Payne distinctly recalled his dick jumping in response.

That keen gaze of hers had gratifyingly explored every inch of him—and, for reasons which escaped him, had seemed particularly impressed with the size of his feet. It had been all he could do not to stand before her and preen like a damned peacock. He knew he owned a certain amount of sex appeal—he'd certainly never had a problem coaxing a woman into bed—but he didn't think he'd ever been the subject of such scrutiny before or obvious…lust, for a lack of better explanation.

She wanted him.

Which was particularly nice, considering he wanted to lay her almost as much as he wanted to wring her delicate little neck. Let her keep up these petty, pointless games and he'd turn the tables on her so fast she wouldn't know what hit her. And it would be him—in the sexual sense.

And they'd *both* enjoy it.

Payne backtracked into the house, explained his unfortunate circumstances and was vastly relieved when Harry, Norah's husband, retrieved a portable compressor from the barn.

Three frustrating hours later he spotted the Hummer at Beauregard's Antique Mall. She was in sight, Payne decided, his lips curling into an evil smile.

Time to let her see what she was up against.

"THIS IS LOVELY," Emma said, handing the last pocketwatch in the case back to the clerk. She heaved a small disappointed sigh. "But it's not exactly what I'm looking for."

Looking a bit disgruntled, the clerk carefully returned the watch to its place beneath the glass. "Well, dear, I'm afraid that's all I can show you here. Perhaps you'll have better luck elsewhere."

He might as well have said, "You've wasted my time, so off you go," and Emma could hardly blame him. He'd followed her around from booth to booth, opening up every case in this particular mall in search of "the perfect pocketwatch." She'd made up a cock-and-bull story about trying to find one similar to the one her grandfather had worn and, initially, every proprietor she'd met up to this point had been thrilled to accommodate her.

But after she systematically culled each and every one, citing vague reasons such as this one's too small, this one's too large, the numbers are wrong, etc…their enthusiasm for the search had, admittedly, waned. It would be considerably easier if she could simply say that she was looking for a gold pocketwatch with the inscription "Lighthorse" on it, but Hastings had warned her against that tack, the theory being that if a dealer had managed to miss the connection to start with, it wouldn't take long to put it together and the price would significantly go up.

It made sense, she supposed, but it didn't make her job any easier. Her lips slid into a wry, satisfied smile. In fact, the only thing that *had* made her job easier today was not having Payne looking over her shoulder every minute.

"What was wrong with that one?" he asked, as though the mere thought of him had conjured him out of thin air.

Emma gasped and all but jumped out of her skin. Pressing her hand to her throat, she whirled on him. "You scared me half to death," she accused, annoyed that she'd allowed him to sneak up on her like that.

Then again, that had been part of his training. Hell, for all she knew, he might have been following her for hours and she simply hadn't known it. It was doubtful—she expected she would have felt a lingering presence—but it wasn't out of the realm of possibility.

"Pity," Payne remarked, that cool unflappable gaze honing in on hers.

"Pity you didn't scare me to death, or pity that you almost did?" she asked, curiously unnerved by his calm demeanor.

"Whichever meaning suits you."

Emma wandered farther down the display case and pretended to be interested in a plate full of Confederate bills. "Having any luck?" she asked lightly.

"It just changed."

Meaning that he'd been looking for her instead of the pocketwatch, which was exactly what she'd been counting on. If she could keep him preoccupied with her instead of their treasure hunt, her chances of beating him to the watch would be greatly improved. She didn't have any idea how long this little ruse would work, but she was going to take advantage of it while she could.

Letting the air out of his tires this morning was

a bit on the drastic side, but the more she'd thought about it last night, the more she'd become convinced that she didn't have a hope in hell of beating him if she simply let him run the show—his usual method of operation. She had to thwart him and if that meant pulling a few low punches, then so be it. He'd been a Ranger after all—a legendary badass. Her lips quirked. He could take it.

Furthermore, with Ranger Security behind him, he had a clear advantage that she didn't possess. Her conscience had screamed the entire time the air had hissed out of the tires—instead of refuting her "ruthless" reputation, she was only confirming it—but, ultimately, she'd mentally muffled the scream by imagining how good it would feel to write out the checks for the past-due bills and pay for that first semester of college.

Clearly he had the money and the means to do what he wanted—had already gotten his post military career off the ground. She wasn't asking for a handout, merely a hand-up, and this opportunity was too good to pass up. She'd be an idiot not to use every means in her limited disposal to make sure that she secured the outcome and thereby, her future.

She wasn't here to make friends, dammit—she was here to win.

"Did you sleep well last night?" Payne asked her.

"Like a baby," she lied, feeling him move even closer behind her. It appeared that now that he'd found her, he wasn't letting her out of his sight. The idea sent a wicked thrill coursing through her and the hair on her arms stood on end.

She caught a hint of a smile in his voice. "You did a lot of rattling around for someone who slept like a baby."

"I'm sorry if I kept you awake."

Another lie. That had been the whole point. She'd catnapped, then made enough noise to intrigue him, then catnapped again. Finally, when she'd heard him get into the shower—a notion that all but made her melt—she'd hurried downstairs, snagged a muffin from Matthew, then let the air out of Payne's tires and left.

Her hands hadn't been altogether steady, but she'd gotten the job done and was actually sort of proud of herself for trumping Garrett's ace on the first hand. Now it was only a matter of keeping it up. He'd be a helluva lot harder to beat the next go-round, she knew, but she'd planned for that and had packed a few accessories accordingly. She'd even borrowed a couple of wigs from her mother's shop just for the occasion.

Knowing that she couldn't disguise the Hummer, it was a good thing she could hide herself. Tomorrow she planned to park the Hummer in town and catch a bus to the rest of her destinations. As for how she was going to give him the slip to start with, she hadn't worked that one out yet.

But she would.

"I guess I should be thankful you didn't slash the tires," Payne said conversationally.

Emma felt her lips twitch. "That would have been overkill. I just needed to slow you down. I thought I made it clear that I didn't want you to follow me yesterday when I tried to avoid you." She shrugged lightly. "You didn't take the hint."

"And I thought I made it clear that I didn't have any intention of letting you avoid me. You don't seem to have grasped that hint, either." She detected a slight throb in his voice, one that made her skin prickle with an odd mixture of warning and desire.

"I've always been very fond of the direct approach," Emma said, turning to face him.

"Fine. I'll be direct. If you continue to sabotage me, I will make you eternally sorry." His lips curled into a smile that never reached his eyes. "How's that for direct?"

Emma's breath had stalled in her lungs, but she managed to find it. "That's pretty damned good. Let me be equally frank. I don't like being followed and if you continue to do so, I will do everything in my power to thwart you, if for no other reason than to see that vein that's currently throbbing in your forehead bulge. Follow me again and I'll not only flatten your tires, I'll climb up there and clobber you with them."

He stared at her for a full three seconds before a startled laugh broke up in his throat. "You'll cl-clobber me?"

She nodded.

Then he lost it, giving in to big, giant belly laughs that caused other patrons to turn and stare. It occurred to Emma that he'd probably never purposely allowed himself to attract that type of attention before. Was he cracking up? she wondered. Had she, of all people, managed to push him too far?

Still chuckling, his eyes twinkling with humor, Payne crowded even farther into her personal space, grabbing her arms and lifting her completely off the floor. Then he planted a long, slow, deliberate kiss that made her toes curl midair and her heart segue into an irregular ridiculously pleased rhythm. The kiss ended as abruptly as it had begun and he promptly set her back on the ground. Thankfully the counter was at her back.

"Clobber me, eh, Little Bit? Now, that I'd love to see."

8

PAYNE WATCHED EMMA ANGLE the Hummer back into the parking lot at The Dove's Nest. Within seconds, she'd swiftly exited the car and hurried up the steps before he could follow her. He could have of course, had he wanted to run, but he figured he'd done a good enough job today of rattling her.

Not to mention himself, but that was a thought for a later time.

Like never.

Self-examination wasn't a favorite pastime of his and Payne had become an expert at avoiding it.

Though she had tried to alternately annoy and ignore him out of existence the rest of the morning and afternoon, Payne had continued to follow her. Granted trying to find the watch and keep up with her wasn't going to be an easy feat, but he couldn't think of any other way to handle things. He needed to know where she'd been—that was actually a handy perk for himself because he didn't have to duplicate her efforts—and if she happened to stumble upon a vital piece of information, then he wanted to know about it.

Despite his late start and his search for Emma-the-pain-in-the-ass, he'd managed to cover a good bit of ground today. Though she didn't realize it, of course, in a roundabout way, she'd actually done him a favor. In his ever-maddening search for her, he'd canvassed the stores she'd missed, so technically speaking, he was ahead of the game. He'd considered pointing this out to Mistress Logic, but was afraid he'd be provoked into kissing her again, so he'd decided against it.

With his world in relatively good order, he'd spent the rest of his day making sure that she was just as miserable and irritated as he'd been this morning. And if he enjoyed himself—immensely—in the process, well then that was all the better.

Payne felt his lips form a self-satisfied smile and strolled up the steps to the front porch. Norah's sister and her large pig—once again garbed in matching ensembles, he noted with a wry twist of his lips—sat in a pair of wicker rockers on the far end of the porch. He mentally shook his head, wondering what would make a person want to own bacon for a pet, much less wrestle it into clothes? It took all types, he supposed.

"Good afternoon," she called with a welcoming smile. "Having a good time in Gettysburg so far?" The ridiculous-looking pig snorted, seemingly echoing the question. Today the couple were outfitted in blue velour spandex, which did nothing to disguise their considerable girth.

Payne nodded. "I am, thanks."

"Glad to hear it." She took a deep breath and gazed out over the grounds as though she saw something he'd failed to notice. "It's been a lovely day."

It had been colder than a witch's tit in a brass bra, but he didn't disagree with her, merely smiled and walked inside. A merry blaze burned in fireplaces in the dining room to the left and the parlor to the right, sending a blanketing warmth from one side of the house to the other.

Looking warm and happy, Harry stood at the antique check-in desk and spoke amiably to someone on the phone, presumably a potential customer. He offered a kind grin and waved at Payne as he walked in. Though it could have only been a product of his imagination, Harry had seemed genuinely happy to see him. Another perk to B&B service, Payne decided, making a mental note to consider checking out other family-run establishments as opposed to a hotel the next time he traveled.

He supposed he'd always considered them a couples-only kind of place—and he'd never been a couples-only kind of guy—but if this was the standard level of service, then he didn't give a damn if he traveled with a significant other or not.

For whatever reason, an image of Emma's elfin face sprang instantly to mind. He'd spent an exorbitant amount of time studying that profile today, had examined it from various vantage points, but the end result was always the same— he found her breathtaking at any angle.

The clean line of her jaw, the smooth roundness of her cheek, the way her sleek dark brows rumpled into an adorable frown when he said something particularly provoking. Those mesmerizing smoky amethyst eyes had the singular ability to make the air thin in his lungs and deliver a blow to his equilibrium that could figuratively knock him off his feet.

And her mouth.

Sweet Lord.

This morning when he'd snapped and kissed her, Payne had known that he'd made a serious tactical error. She'd tasted like hot tea and oranges. And the first feel of those ripe, soft lips against his had made his knees quake and his stomach slide into a violent, unexpected tailspin.

If looking into those eyes the first time had rocked his foundation, then kissing her had fractured it.

While Payne had never been the player Jamie had been before he married, or the girl-magnet Guy's irreverent Maverick-like style attitude had always drawn, he'd nevertheless had his share of attention from the opposite sex. Quite honestly, he'd gotten more attention than he'd wanted, given that all he was interested in was a thorough tumble and a clean, uncomplicated goodbye immediately afterward.

He had never spent the entire night with a woman and, unless he just completely lost his mind or became incapacitated, never intended to. Aside from being a Bachelor's League mandate, there was something too intimate about the act. An implied trust he'd never achieved.

Like any red-blooded man, he had a considerable sex drive and enjoyed the soft pleasures of a woman's body as much as the next guy. Furthermore, given his type A predilections, the idea of not being at the top of his game in any area was unacceptable.

That included lovemaking.

Over the years he'd amassed quite a repertoire of skills when it came to bed play. Though he looked forward to the promise of an orgasm, Payne had mastered the art of delaying climax until after his partner had achieved it—it was bad form to leave a girl in the lurch, after all—and he hadn't suffered any sort of close call or otherwise in years.

Until today.

Simply kissing Emma Langsford—the bane of his recent existence—had, unbelievably, initiated the launch sequence and if he hadn't put her down when he had, Payne grimly suspected he would have made a noticeable mess in his jeans. As it was, she couldn't have failed to notice the bulge in the front of them because he was relatively certain she'd felt it. Gratifyingly, she'd tried to wiggle closer to him. Payne would have liked nothing better than to have plopped her delectable bottom on top of a display case and taken her until her screaming orgasm milked his loins and she no longer had any doubt that *he* was in charge. He frowned broodingly.

Clearly she was missing that particular point.

Hours later, he still couldn't explain his actions. One minute he'd been standing there, seething, and the next, when she'd made that ridiculous comment about "climbing up there and clobbering him"— *her? Little, tiny* her *an actual match for him?*—he'd been struck dumb by the incongruity of it all, and he'd done the first thing which had come to mind. He'd lifted her up and planted a kiss on that arrogant, outrageous, sinfully beautiful mouth of hers.

The new challenge, of course, would be not doing it again.

Frankly, for the first time in his life, Payne was worried about keeping his so-called iron will in control. He'd lost it more times in the last twenty-four hours than he had in his entire life. Emma was gorgeous and intriguing, witty and ruthless, sexy and vulnerable and something about the combination made him forget about being on guard. It made him want to know her better, of all damn things, when he shouldn't give a damn about her one way or the other. It made him want to believe in the inherent goodness he saw in her, in addition to the drive.

He wasn't merely intrigued. Intrigue he could handle. Intrigue left him interested but still able to utilize good judgment. Unfortunately he'd bypassed intrigue and had gone directly into obsessed.

Dangerous waters, he knew, and with every passing minute in her company he felt himself wading further away from the bank of his own self-control.

He only hoped, when the moment came, that he'd remember how to swim.

Atlanta

"PAYNE'S IN TROUBLE," Jamie announced with a bewildered scowl as he holstered his cell phone. The noise inside Samuel's Pub, their usual beer and sandwich hangout, had forced him to take the call outside and he'd only just returned.

Guy looked up from his hot wings and went on instant alert. "What do you mean?"

"I mean, I don't know who this chick is, but—" he started chuckling "—she's completely knocked him off his game. She gave him the slip this morning."

Guy stilled and felt a slow disbelieving smile slide across his lips. "You're shittin' me."

"No, I'm not," he said, plopping back down

into his chair. "Don't let me forget to take Audrey those hot wings she asked for," he said absently. "She'll kill me if I come back empty-handed."

Guy doubted that, but he had witnessed a particularly ugly mood swing from the usually even-tempered Mrs. Flanagan this morning, so he supposed it could happen. People had snapped over less, he knew. "Payne actually told you that? That Emma had given him the slip?"

"Not initially," Jamie said. "I could tell that he wasn't in his regular dry ice form, so I kept pushing until he had to tell me."

That made more sense. Payne actually admitting to a failure of any kind had to be difficult, especially since, to Guy's knowledge, his cool-headed friend had never made a mistake in his life. "How'd she do it?"

"She kept him up all night, waited for him to get in the shower and then made her escape."

Guy selected an onion ring. "I warned him about her. She's got a reputation for being relentless."

"That could simply be sour grapes from guys she's bested," Jamie scoffed, playing devil's advocate. "You know better than to listen to rumors. Would Hastings have sent her if she wasn't a good choice?"

He supposed not. Still... Any woman who could trip up Brian Payne bore watching closely. "Has he asked for help?"

Jamie took a swig of his Guinness. "No and I got the impression that he doesn't want any. I don't think he wants to have an unfair advantage by utilizing our services."

Guy smirked and shook his head. Noble bastard. Now that was the difference between the two of them. If he'd been in Payne's position, he'd have everybody at Ranger Security helping him out. He'd use every possible advantage he had and wouldn't give a damn whether it was fair or not. He'd complete the mission using any means possible, simply to be done with it. Half of Guy's mouth hitched up in a grin. But that wasn't The Specialist's style. He'd always been so damned good at everything that he hadn't had to get creative to make the end justify the means. Yet.

Another thought struck him. "If he doesn't want our help, why did he call?"

Jamie chuckled. "Why the hell do you think? Just checking in, making sure everything is running smoothly in his absence."

That figured, Guy thought, not the least bit

insulted. Guy knew it was killing Payne to be away, to surrender control of Ranger Security to the two of them. Payne had always been a control freak, but Guy and Jamie had both noticed that their friend seemed to have gotten worse since Danny's death.

First he'd thrown himself into getting out of the military and then he'd thrown himself into building Ranger Security and handling the renovations on their building and apartments. Knowing that he'd needed the distraction, Guy and Jamie had merely stepped back and let Payne manage—it was what he did best, after all. Handling the details had been Payne's Novocaine. Until he'd found Audrey, sex had been Jamie's.

Guy had merely plowed ahead and hadn't looked for a painkiller. He didn't deserve one. He just planned to meet each day with the same stoic resolve he had since Danny had died, to deal with having the death of a friend on his hands as a deserved penance for his mistake.

Like Jamie and Payne, he wanted to get his favor to Garrett over with, wanted that last tie to the military and that life he'd had before severed for good. But while he knew that Jamie had found peace after his mission was completed—with

Audrey's help, of course—and he suspected that Payne would be able to let go of some of his own guilt as a result of completing his last favor, Guy didn't hold out any such hope. The ultimate forgiveness would have to come from within and he knew he'd never reach that place. How could he, when things had gone so terribly wrong? When, as senior officer, he'd been the one in charge and had gotten his friend killed?

"Emma Langsford sounds familiar," Jamie commented.

"Maybe you slept with her," Guy said, ribbing his friend about his prior sexual habits.

"Shut up, you bastard," Jamie told him, chuckling. "I'm serious. I've heard of her."

"She was Hastings's 'go-to' girl. Like I said, she developed a reputation for being relentless, unpredictable and very, very lucky."

Jamie shot him speculative smile. "I remember hearing about her. She reminded me of someone at the time."

Guy frowned. "How could she remind you of someone when you've never met her?"

"I've met her type."

"Her type?"

Jamie took another drink and his lips slid into

an unrepentant grin. "Right. She's the feminine version of *you*."

Guy chuckled, recognizing the truth. "Well, I'll be damned," he said.

Jamie grunted. "Let's just hope Payne isn't."

9

"ANY LUCK YET?" Colonel Hastings asked.

Emma shouldered the phone, stood up and crammed her feet back into her shoes. After the wearing afternoon—not to mention *The Kiss*—her nerves had been frayed to the breaking point and she'd needed a long soak in a hot bubble bath for some perspective and a little time looking at the backs of her eyelids to recuperate.

Perspective had been a no-show, but she did feel marginally rested after her brief nap. In fact, if Hastings hadn't called for a "status report" she'd undoubtedly still be snoozing.

"Not yet, sir," Emma told him. Hell, she'd only been here a little over a day and had been having to contend with Payne—literally and figuratively—during that time. Sheesh. Surely he hadn't expected immediate results. If the damned watch hadn't been found in roughly 140 years, wasn't it a tad unreasonable to expect her to locate it in less than twenty-four hours?

"No worries," Hastings assured her. "I'm sure you'll find it first. Have you run into Major Payne yet?"

Yes, Emma thought, letting go a shaky breath. Directly into his lips. Oy, mercy, but could the man kiss. "He's staying at this B&B, as well," Emma told him.

Hastings laughed. "You're right under his nose then. Does he have any idea who you are?"

"Yes, sir. He does."

"Damn," he swore, suddenly deflated. "How did he find out?"

Emma glossed over her taking the Hummer part, which she was sure had ultimately outed her, and mentioned the Ranger Security connection instead. "This would have been helpful information to have," she added, unable to disguise the slightly perturbed growl in her voice.

"I was concerned that you'd be intimidated if you knew what line of work Payne had gone into post-military."

Be that as it may, he still should have told her. But she wasn't interested in arguing the point. She'd already made hers.

Instead, she quickly brought him up to speed on her progress. "I've covered the majority of the antique stores in and around town today, and am going to hit the rest tomorrow. If that search proves futile, then I'm going to go ahead and start sifting through the list of names from the auction house you've given me."

"Sounds like an excellent plan, Emma. Let me know how it goes. And don't let Payne intimidate you. He's just a man, after all, and you've proven you're a worthy opponent for one of those before, haven't you?"

Emma felt a smile tug at her lips, heartened by his confidence. "Yes, sir."

"That's my girl." And with that parting comment, he disconnected.

Though, like Payne, she didn't appreciate the bet part of Hastings's and Garrett's machinations, she couldn't deny that she had a lot of respect for Colonel Hastings and genuinely appreciated the opportunity he'd given her to finance her way into a better life.

Provided she found the pocketwatch first, she would be shaving off at least three years of hard work and getting into vet school that much faster. Honestly, without this new start, who knew if she'd have ever gotten the chance? She'd like to think so—she'd always been determined—but the possibility of scratching the dream off as a lost cause or too expensive might have proved tempting. At any rate, love him or hate him, she appreciated the Hastings offer regardless of what Payne thought of the bet.

Or, as much as she wished she didn't care, what he would ultimately think of her.

If she'd been a guy, no doubt he would have decked her instead of kissing her this morning. But since she'd been a woman and she'd pushed him past his coping point, he'd done the first thing he could think of to put her in her place—he'd lifted her right off the floor and kissed her—and if they'd been anywhere but in a public place, he would have had her on her back three minutes later. Perversely, she found herself disappointed that he hadn't.

Honestly, Emma thought. The way she'd reacted, you'd think she'd never been kissed before. Her silly heart had done a little cartwheel of joy, her bones had melted and every hair on her body had prickled as though she'd been hit with a slight electric charge. It had been a take-no-prisoners, shut-up-or-put-out siege that had absolutely rocked her world and shaken her senses.

Or made her sense*less,* as the case may be, she thought with a wry smile. Because all she'd been able to think about since he'd ended the kiss was pissing him off enough to get another one.

And another one.

On her neck, her breasts, and needy, equally sensitive places farther south.

In her secret fantasies about the legendary so-cool-he-was-hot former Ranger, Emma had always imagined him being a thorough and methodical lover. She'd imagined him taking his time, lingering, if you will, from one end of her body to the other. Inspecting, measuring, kissing, sucking and stroking her. Coaxing a flame, stoking a fire to a slow but steady fever pitch of sexual satisfaction. It had been a fabulous fantasy, complete with the occasional help-yourself orgasm on her part.

Now she had to revise her fantasy and, though she wouldn't have thought it possible, she preferred the new one to the old. The new one featured a so-cool-he-was-hot legendary badass former Ranger coming *unglued*—for her.

That kiss might have started out as a lesson for her—but it had swiftly morphed into something else altogether. His tongue hadn't asked for entrance—it had *demanded* it. She'd tasted the need there, the sweet flavor of wild, primal desire and her own body had reacted in kind. An uncontrollable urge had spiked in her loins, licked through her veins, burning up any vestiges of ordinary sexual hunger. She'd wanted to devour him and, given that mouthwatering enormous bulge she'd felt against her belly, he'd been equally as hungry for her.

As if things hadn't been complicated enough, Emma thought with a helpless whimper. Now he had to go and throw that damned kiss into the mix. The kiss that made her want *so* much more.

It gave an entirely new meaning to sleeping with the enemy.

Emma's stomach rumbled, reminding her of yet another hunger which hadn't been satisfied today. Certain she wouldn't have been able to get a raisin down her throat with a slingshot while she and Payne were joined at the hip—or at the ass, since he'd mostly followed her—Emma had elected not to stop for lunch, but had continued her search instead.

Naturally, he'd been above something as trivial as food, so they'd plowed on throughout the day without stopping for so much as a sandwich. Thankfully she still had a couple of cookies left in her room from yesterday and had washed them down with a bottle of water she'd carried in her purse. But one muffin and two cookies didn't a proper meal make and she was hungry. Norah, bless her accommodating heart, had flagged her down when she'd rushed back in this afternoon long enough to tell her that dinner would be ready at six.

Emma glanced at the clock and saw that it was five minutes, to the hour. Close enough, she thought with a sigh, pushing up from her bed. No doubt Payne would be in the dining room already, but maybe she'd get lucky and end up seated on the opposite side of the room. The opposite side of the planet would probably be better for her sexual sanity, but that was too much to hope for.

She ran her fingers through her hair, fluffing it a little to get rid of the bed-head, and fumbled through her purse for her compact. A little powder, a little gloss—God help her, Emma thought, realizing she was doing the frou-frou thing because Payne was more than likely downstairs. Sheesh. Disgusted with herself, she jammed the cap back on her lipstick and tossed it back into her bag. She was an idiot—an absolute idiot—and, as a bracing act of defiance, she immediately wiped off the newly applied gloss.

Muttering under her breath, she snagged her purse and walked downstairs.

"Ah," Norah said as she approached the dining room. "You're here."

"And very hungry," Emma added with a significant grin. "Something smells good."

"Dad made pot roast. It's *fabulous*."

It certainly smelled fabulous, Emma thought, her mouth watering.

"Come with me," she said, herding Emma forward into the dining area. "Your dinner companion is already seated. I've paired you up with the best-looking man here. With the exception of my husband, of course," she added with a knowing twinkle.

Emma's gaze tangled with Payne's from across the room and she felt a sick smile catch the corner of her mouth and tug. "Oh, how nice," she said, because an "Oh, shit," didn't seem appropriate. "Did he ask you to do this?" she prompted, trying to sound secretly thrilled as opposed to ready to wretch. She wouldn't put it past him in the least.

"It was my suggestion, but he was quite pleased with it."

She'd just bet he was, Emma thought, inwardly seething.

"I think he may like you," Norah confided, her gaze warm. "We've had more than one couple begin their romance here."

Romance? Her and Brian Payne?

Emma's heart gave an odd little jolt and a nervous chill hit her belly. Now, that was certainly a frightening thought, one her foolish heart thankfully had sense enough not to entertain.

Now…sleeping with him? Sure, she could do that. It would be mutually satisfying, and everybody would go home happy. But falling for him? Saying, "Here's my heart, please don't flashfreeze and break it?"

Absolutely not.

In the first place, she knew what a hardened bachelor looked like, and he was *it* if she'd ever seen one. A man didn't manage to get to the ripe of age of thirtysomething as a bachelor without a reason. He was either vehemently opposed to the idea, had commitment issues or was gay. She could personally rule out the latter and pegged him for a mutant combination of the other two.

And in the second place, a guy with those kinds of issues—particularly one with Payne's considerable fortitude—was more than she reasonably imagined she could tackle. The temptation was there, of course. He'd be a challenge. But she instinctively knew that if she dared to offend him with any kind of tender emotion, he'd freeze her out so fast her hair would turn to ice. Risking her heart while knowing the outcome would be emotional suicide and frankly, all recklessness aside, even *she* had better sense than that.

Pity though, Emma thought as she made her way across the dining room. If he ever cared enough to focus some of the legendary attention-to-detail on loving a woman, she'd be one lucky girl.

For whatever reason, the idea was wholly depressing.

Possibly because she knew that girl would never be her.

PAYNE FELT his lips slide into a smirk as Emma took the seat opposite him. "Haven't lost your appetite, have you?"

She placed her napkin in her lap, then looked up and blinked at him. "Why would I do that?"

"Oh, I don't know." He took a hefty drink of wine, hoping to drown some of the irritation he was feeling. "I guess because you looked nauseous a moment ago when you saw me sitting here."

"Have I hurt your feelings?" she asked with mock concern, being her typical smart-ass self. The galling answer was yes, but he'd rather have his balls sawed off with a pair of dull hedge clippers than tell her that. Furthermore, he wasn't supposed to have feelings for her to hurt, so that telling realization made him distinctly uncomfortable.

"No, I'd just prefer you not puke on *my* food," he drawled, purposely sounding uninterested. "So long as you're just sick of my company and not *sick,* we should be fine."

Emma paused to look at him and he had the momentary uneasy sensation that she'd somehow picked up on the lie. That she could see through him. She rolled her eyes, looking miserably contrite. "I'm not sick of you, per se," she told him and gestured wearily. "I'm just sick of…the tension, if that makes sense."

Of the sexual variety? he wondered, or of the find-the-pocketwatch kind?

In either case, he knew what she meant. After all, it was only Day Two and he felt as if he'd been through a week of hell. His broody gaze swung back to Emma.

And it was all her fault.

Women, he thought darkly, the historical

downfall of all the men in his family. But no matter how much she mucked up his game, she wouldn't be *his* downfall. In fact, if this mission played out as successfully as every other one in his life had, then it would be the other way around.

For whatever reason, that thought wasn't as comforting as it should have been. He supposed because in this instance, he wasn't busting up a terrorist cell or freeing prisoners of war. He was here on another man's whim, protecting his honor for the sake of a historical trinket whose actual authenticity was still in question. There was no honor in this errand, no greater good to be won and, in this case, winning meant making sure somebody lost. Her.

Time to mine for a little more information in that regard, Payne thought, telling himself it was strictly for professional reasons. So he'd be better armed and all that. It couldn't possibly be because he was fascinated by her and wanted to know everything she'd willingly share about herself. That would be pathetic and Brian Atticus Payne was not, under any circumstances, *pathetic*.

"What do you say we call a brief truce?"

She cocked her head and regarded him through cautious eyes. "How brief?"

"Dinner," he replied. "Let's just eat and be cordial. Do you think you can do that?"

Her lips twitched. "If I put my mind to it."

Payne snorted. God, she was adorable.

Emma released a small breath and relaxed back into her chair, seemingly at a loss now that she was supposed to be nice to him. She folded her hands primly in her lap and he watched her gaze dart around the dining room, evidently prepared to look at anything but him. She almost appeared…nervous, but that hardly fit the balls-to-the-wall little spitfire he'd come to know.

"So," he said, deciding to toss an old line into the conversational pond, "what made you decide to join the military?"

That violet gaze finally found his and her lips slid into an endearing, self-deprecating smile. "A dare."

He chewed the inside of his cheek to hide his smile. "A dare?"

She nodded. "Hardly the noble reason I'm sure you joined. You probably had grandiose notions about God and country, protecting our borders and freedoms." She paused while Harry slid steaming plates filled with pot roast, potatoes, carrots and onions in front of them. "While I, on the other hand, let some bone-headed guy taunt me into it. I joined simply to prove a point."

Given his recent encounters with her, he could easily see that. "I take it you proved that point."

She quirked an eyebrow. "I served eight years. What do you think?"

He barely knew her and, oddly, wouldn't expect anything less. "Eight years, eh?"

"Yeah," she confessed with a wistful sigh. "I would have re-upped, but my grandfather was dying and my mother needed me at home."

"I'm sorry."

She lifted her shoulders in a small shrug. "Ah, well. You do what you've got to do, eh? Family comes first."

He wouldn't know anything about that, because his had always been a dys*fuck*tional mess, to borrow Guy's word for it. Still, it was reaffirming to see that some families were normal, or had achieved an approximation thereof, at any rate. An unexpected pang of wistfulness for that kind of bond washed over him—odd, when he thought he'd beaten that longing into submission years ago—but he managed to wrestle it away with images of his feuding, miserable parents.

"So what's next for you?" Payne asked.

"You're mother had mentioned something about vet school to Guy."

She smiled. "She thought he was a potential boyfriend. She would have told him that I was out saving kittens from a drainage pipe if she'd thought it would have made me seem more attractive."

Payne felt a laugh break up in his throat. Finished eating, his pushed his plate away. "So she was lying?"

"About vet school? No. I want to go. It's Plan C."

Thoroughly intrigued, he leaned back in his chair and sipped his wine. "What happened to plans A and B?"

"A was the military. It didn't pan out." A wry smile ripened her lips. "Right now, Plan B constitutes checking groceries at the Hefty Hog and picking up every bit of work I can until I can afford Plan C." Her brow clouded. "My grandfather's care was…a strain. I'm helping my mother out right now."

Payne stilled, digesting that little bit of information. So it was as bad as Guy had said, possibly even worse. Hastings's timely offer had been a much-needed shot of financial breathing room, and the only thing standing between her and a better life was him. He'd known this, of course, but he hadn't fully absorbed it until now. Something about her glib, resigned tone made the enormity of what she stood to lose if he won all the more stark and ugly.

"Having an attack of nobility?" she drawled, utilizing that uncanny method she had of reading his thoughts when no one else, even his closest friends, had ever been able to do so.

"No," Payne lied, slightly perturbed.

"Good. Don't. It's insulting."

"Insulting?"

"That's right." She regarded him with cool amusement. "It implies that you actually don't think I can find the pocketwatch before you do— that I am incapable—and *that,* Sir Brainiac, is insulting."

A smile meandered across his lips. "I take it we're finished being cordial."

She grimaced adorably, then grinned. "Cordial's boring. I'd much rather fight with you."

And he'd much rather take her to bed, but that was hardly polite dinner conversation, now was it? "I'd finished eating, anyway," Payne said.

"Good. Then I didn't break any rules."

No, she just liked bending them shy of breaking

them—just like Guy, Payne realized with an uneasy start. Now that was a comparison he should have made before now, he thought, not altogether sure he liked the similarity. Before he could articulate a response, she stood.

"This wasn't so bad," she said. "Maybe we should do it again sometime."

"Back to being a smart-ass, I see," Payne remarked, shooting her a long-suffering look as he stood.

She batted her lashes at him. "It's part of my charm."

"You should slap whoever told you that."

"Bite your tongue," she admonished with a patently false frown. "I'd never hit my mother."

"Come on," he said. "I'll walk you up."

"There you go again. I think I know the way."

"I didn't say you didn't. I was being a gentleman," he said through partially gritted teeth. Good Lord, she seemed determined to step on each and every one of his already shredded nerves.

"Oh. Well, thank you, then. I wasn't aware I was in the company of one." She mounted the stairs, then turned and faced him at the top of the landing with an exaggerated frown. "Was that what you were being when you picked me up off the floor today and kissed me without permission?" she asked innocently. She fished out her key from her purse and started toward her door.

Payne's face burned. "Sorry. My mistake," he said tightly. "I must have misinterpreted your tongue in my mouth."

She unlocked her door, but didn't open it, then turned around and glared at him from between narrowed eyes. "It was a reflex."

A reflex, eh? Payne thought, goaded—*drawn*—into her personal space once more. He was being a bully again, but he couldn't seem to help himself. She did that to him. Made him act first and think later.

He backed her into her door, forcing her to look up at him, and braced his hands on either side of her head, effectively boxing her in. Her eyes widened and a wild pulse fluttered at the base of her throat. "Does that mean you'd *reflexively* kiss me back if I did it again?" he asked softly, lowering his head.

He stopped a hairbreadth away from her mouth, could taste her sweet breath, but purposely didn't close the distance between them, forcing her to make the call. Her gaze tangled with his—hot, hungry, desperate and torn—then drifted down to his lips once more. Another one of her sighs caressed his lips, then she whimpered, said, "To hell with it." And then kissed him as if her very life depended on it.

10

I AM SUCH A MORON, Emma told herself as she wrapped her arms around Payne's neck and her legs around his waist. In the nanosecond after she decided to accept his dare—because that had been what it was and the self-serving wretch knew she couldn't resist, dammit—and had closed the paper-thin distance between their mouths, Payne had scooped her up and was feeding at her mouth as though she was a feast and he hadn't eaten in…forever.

Her back banged against the door, forcing a startled oomph from her mouth, which he promptly savored. With one powerful arm wrapped around her waist, she felt him fumble for the doorknob behind him. The latch gave way and he stumbled forward, his mouth never leaving hers. Utterly on fire for each other, he kicked the door shut with his foot and they bounced off walls and furniture like human pinballs at the mercy of the paddles in a machine. It was mindless and thrilling and every cell in her body rejoiced with the sheer madness of what was to come.

Namely her.

Emma clawed open his shirt, then trailed a desperate kiss down the side of his jaw and onto his neck. She wanted to taste him everywhere. The sweet salty tang of his skin exploded on her tongue, making her senses sing with wild, uncontrollable need.

Payne's big hands cupped her bottom, aligning her along the hard, jutting ridge of his arousal and he flexed against her, forcing a gasp of sheer delight out of her mouth. Her feminine muscles clenched, coating her folds with hot joy juice and her clit tingled with an achy heavy heat. She drew back long enough to tug her shirt over her head and cast it aside, and a second later, they were tumbling onto the bed. She felt it shift as he landed beside her. He was big and strong, a modern warrior, and for the moment, totally *hers*.

She almost came, just thinking about it.

Payne's hot breath slipped over her ear, eliciting a shiver, then his tongue licked a hot path along the side of her neck. Her lids fluttered, drunk with sensation, with the scent of Man and arousal and a woodsy fragrance that was all his. Meanwhile, one hand had found her breast and was thumbing her budded nipple through the gauzy material of her bra.

Desperate for the feel of him, Emma grabbed the back of his shirt and pulled it up and over his head. The bedside lamp illuminated broad, sleek shoulders and muscles upon muscles, the perfect male form, and for one heart-stopping moment all she could do was stare…and enjoy. Her palms found his chest, slid over each and every ridge and valley, savoring the feel of his warm supple skin.

His dog tags dangled between them and a tattoo of an eagle with a ribbon and the inscription *In Memory of Danny Boy* trailing from its beak had been inked upon his chest, directly over his heart. Her own heart squeezed for him, suddenly remembering that he'd lost a friend a little over a year ago. Danny Levinson. She had a vague memory of curly auburn hair, green eyes and a mischievous smile. It must have been a lot harder for Payne than she realized, Emma thought, if he'd inked a permanent memorial onto his skin. She frowned, suddenly—

"Don't," he said, then popped the front clasp of her bra.

Emma shivered as her bound breasts suddenly broke free. "Don't what?"

"Analyze me." A soft smile slid over his lips as he looked at her, making her belly all warm and muddled. "It's insulting."

Emma chuckled, recognizing the phrase. Then his hot mouth closed upon her puckered nipple and all thoughts of his fallen friend and the touching tattoo fled from her mind.

She could only feel.

And it was *amazing*.

He suckled first one breast and then the other. He'd take long deep pulls into his mouth, then lave the bud and whisper a breath across the wet peak, making her shiver. He might have been playing at her breasts, but she felt a corresponding tug deep in her womb, most particularly in the heart of her sex. It was as though a tiny thread connected the two, and by the time his talented fingers had slid down her belly, unbuttoned her jeans and forced them over her hips, Emma's panties were drenched.

She felt his fingers slide under the elastic, then part her curls and the first brush of his thumb over her clit had her arching up against him, a silent plea for more.

He instantly accommodated.

"Mmm," he murmured. "So wet."

She pushed shamelessly against his fingers, bent forward and nipped at his shoulder, then kissed the spot she'd bitten. Gratifyingly, she felt his dick jump against her thigh and a satisfied smile slid across her lips. Emma quickly found the snap of his jeans and pulled the button from its closure. His zipper sang, opening his pants wider so that she could work them off his lean hips. Multitasking, she dragged his boxers right along with them. Payne lifted himself up, then shucked them off where they landed at the foot of the bed.

Mercy.

Brian Payne. Gloriously naked, grandly proportioned.

He was huge and magnificent and so beautiful it made her chest ache and her belly tip in a wild delighted roll of sexual pleasure. He *was* a stallion, Emma thought, her mouth alternately drying then watering. She abruptly rolled him onto his back, licked a path over his nipples, suckled him and smiled against him as a startled hiss tore from his lips. She mapped his chest, her hands greedy for the feel of him—latent power, honed to perfection. Sweet God, she wanted him.

"Tell me you have a condom," she all but whimpered, realizing for the first time that she didn't. She wrapped her hand around his dick and worked the slippery skin against her palm. Silk over steel.

Payne winced with pleasure. "In. My. Wallet."

Emma snagged his jeans and threw them toward him. "Get it," she ordered, mesmerized and focused on the part of him she wanted the most. Between her legs. "I'm playing." Then she bent her head and pulled as much of him as she could into her mouth. Smooth as satin, he felt wonderful beneath her tongue.

Payne bucked beneath her and his thighs tensed. "Woman," he growled, seemingly startled.

Still tasting him—licking, laving and loving every inch of him—she looked up, his pulsing dick in her mouth, and her gaze tangled with his. Blue fire burned from his gaze, emboldening her even more. She ran her tongue over the engorged head, sucked up the bead of moisture leaking from there and smiled at him. "What?"

A broken chuckle bubbled up Payne's throat and he tossed the condom toward her. "Here."

Emma tore into the little package, pulled the condom out, then licked him again just for good measure. She heard him growl, and the masculine sound sizzled through her. "It'll go on easier if it's wet."

She swiftly rolled it into place, then settled herself on top of him. That first image she'd had of riding him flashed through her mind, drawing a smile as she slid her drenched sex over him, coating him in her own juices. The head of his penis bumped her aching clit, making her breath hitch in her throat. Reading her, Payne grasped her hips and bumped her again.

Emma pushed harder against him, braced her hands on his chest and absorbed the feeling. God, he was breathtaking. Hands down the most beautiful, sexy man she'd ever seen. And he was at her mercy, allowing her to dominate when she was certain he wanted to roll her over and take control. It was what he was accustomed to, after all, she thought, practically drunk with the power she evidently had over him.

She scored his chest with her nails, then lifted her hips and impaled herself upon him. Her vision blackened around the edges and her belly deflated in a whoosh of startled air. *Sweet heaven,* Emma thought, as indescribable pleasure bolted through her.

Payne's lips peeled back from his teeth and, though it could have only been her imagination, she thought she heard his teeth crack. He flexed beneath her and she could tell that he was holding back, that he was afraid he would hurt her.

"You're so tiny," he said, confirming her thoughts.

Emma lifted her hips once more, then slid down the length of him, savoring every inch, every vibration between their joined bodies. "Don't baby me," she said, upping the tempo, riding him harder, the way she'd wanted to since the first moment she laid eyes on him. "It's insulting."

A flash of respect lit those blue-flame eyes and then a wicked smile caught the corner of his mouth. "Sorry," he said. "I'll—" He caught her rhythm, then bent forward and caught her nipple deep into his mouth "—try not to offend you."

Emma laughed, feeling the first spark of climax ripen in her sex. She tightened her feminine muscles around him, pumped harder and harder, creating a delicious drag and draw between their bodies. Evidently realizing that she was skating the edge of a violent orgasm, he bucked beneath her, then reached between them and massaged her clit.

She shattered.

Emma's mouth opened in a soundless scream and her body bowed from the shock of release. So weak she couldn't move, Payne kept up the tempo beneath her, and every thrust of him deep inside her intensified the contractions.

She collapsed on top of him, certain that she would never be able to move again, and it was at that precise moment that he flipped her over onto her belly, dragged her hips off the mattress and plowed into her from behind. Emma gasped, her body instinctively priming for him again. He pumped harder and harder, his heavy testicles slapping against her aching flesh. It was raw and savage and thrilling and she wanted him to do it to her all night. She grunted and mewled, backed against him as he dove deeper into her body.

He made masculine sounds of pleasure, and she could feel him getting closer and closer to his own release. Impossibly, he seemed to grow even more inside of her and every hot, electrifying inch magnified her own pleasure. Whoever said size didn't matter had never had sex with a man like Brian Payne, Emma decided. Her body made only enough room to hold him tightly and she wanted him to stay there, to remain lodged deep inside of her until the world stopped or time ended. She didn't care. He filled her up so completely she didn't think she'd ever feel empty again.

His arm tightened like a band around her belly and she felt him tense behind her. He made a deep growling noise low in his throat and pumped wildly, in and out, in and out, until suddenly, without warning, she came again. The tide of release pulled her under, then lifted her up. She screamed his name and floated along the waves of bliss.

Her orgasm triggered his own and she felt him seat himself firmly inside of her. He held on to her, grew still as the climax tore through his loins and pulsed inside of her. She felt the warmth of his seed pool in the end of the condom against her womb. The heat detonated another little sparkler of pleasure and she instinctively tightened around him.

Payne kissed the middle of her back, made a grunt of pleasure, then carefully withdrew. He grabbed a tissue from the nightstand and discarded the condom, then breathing heavily, pulled her against his side.

Her gaze tangled with his and she smiled, unable to help herself. Things had just gotten a lot more complicated, but at the moment she didn't give a damn. She was skating the high of *amazing* sex and Payne was looking at her with a bewildered, heavy-lidded steamy gaze that made her heart do an odd little figure eight.

"That was—"

"Incredible," Payne finished.

"I can come up with my own adjectives, thank you very much," Emma told him.

"Shut up."

"What?"

"Shut up. If you talk, we'll fight and—" he laid an arm over his eyes and chuckled softly "—I don't have the strength at the moment to tangle with you."

So she'd worn him out. Immensely pleased with herself, Emma snuggled against his chest and let go a small sigh. Fatigue dragged at her lids. "Fine," she relented with a yawn. "We'll call another truce. But…just a short…one."

Payne breathed into her hair. "I can be cordial if I put my mind to it."

She smiled against his chest and fell asleep.

PAYNE CAME AWAKE with a violent jolt. Dressed in a robe, her hair wet—evidently from a shower— Emma stood over him. "Sorry," she said. "I shouldn't have poked you so hard, but I couldn't get you to wake up. Shouldn't you be getting to your room now?"

Poked him? Getting to his room? Disoriented, Payne glanced around the room, realized it wasn't his and a fraction of a second later—long enough for his face to heat—everything came rushing back to him. The meal, the sex. Emma's hot little body astride his, her plump naked breasts, her body absorbing the force of his thrusts, not to mention the most powerful orgasm he'd ever experienced in his life. His dick stirred, just thinking about it.

The last thing he remembered was pulling her to his side, telling her to shut up, and then drifting off to sleep. That he'd fallen asleep at all was astonishing—he'd never actually *slept* with another person—but that he'd fallen into a deep enough sleep to miss her getting out of the bed, taking a shower, then having to actually *poke* him to wake him up…

That was out of the realm of his immediate understanding and so far out of character, Payne wondered if he'd been possessed or had begun to suffer from multiple personality disorder.

Furthermore, it was humiliating.

He looked up and his bleary gaze connected

with her expectant one. She stood over him, patiently waiting for him to get out of her bed and go to his own room. She'd had her fun and was kicking him out, sending him on his way as though he were a toy she'd grown weary of playing with. If he hadn't been so damned mortified, he'd be pissed. As it was, he had no one to blame but himself. When you're dumb you gotta be tough. He levered up into a sitting position.

"I've gathered your clothes," she said, indicating the neat pile in the chair.

How sweet of her, Payne thought. *Here's your hat, what's your hurry?* He stood and had the privilege of watching those deep blue eyes of hers darken with appreciation as he strolled naked across the room. She might want him to leave, but at least she still *wanted* him. She was still affected by him, much the same way he was by her, and he hadn't imagined or dreamed the wild, fantastic gorilla sex they'd just had. Considering the iffy state of his mind, he hadn't ruled out the possibility.

Payne slipped his boxers back on, but didn't bother to don the rest of his clothes. What was the point? He needed to shower before he could go to bed, and— His gaze slid to hers as a thought struck. The last time he'd showered, she'd taken off and he'd spent an inordinate amount of time looking for her. Was that her plan now? Payne wondered. Is that why she was so matter-of-factly suggesting that he go to his own room? So that she could wait for him to get in the shower and then give him the slip again?

He glanced at the clock—four-thirty. It certainly wasn't out of the realm of possibility. She'd rolled out by five-thirty yesterday morning. In fact, if he was to walk across the hall and get into the shower, that gave her just enough time to finish getting dressed—she'd had her bath, after all, the efficient wench—grab a bite to eat and make her escape.

He toyed with the idea of taking her again, but realized he'd only carried one condom with him and they'd used it. He made a mental note to stop by the drugstore at some point today and buy a box. His broody gaze drifted over her, lingered along the smooth curve of her cheek, her plump suckable lips. She wore a pink chenille robe which was easily a size too big because several inches of the hem dragged along the ground and a soft tropical scent flavored the air. She smelled like coconut and pineapple, fresh and ripe and ready to eat.

She'd eaten him, he remembered—vividly.

Honestly, watching her mouth close over his dick, her tongue dart out and capture the single bead he'd allowed to leak out and then watching the audacious creature look up at him from between his legs had to be *the* singular most sexy thing he'd ever seen. She was bold and confident and fearless and she made love with the kind of animalistic abandon that most guys only dreamed about, but never got to experience.

Emma Langsford was one of those rare individuals who did nothing in half measures. Whatever she set her mind to held her full attention and she enthusiastically tackled everything with the same driven fervor. No wonder Hastings had sent her here, Payne thought. He knew his own worth, knew that he was cool-headed, methodical and focused. But she was…ruthless, in a good way.

Nevertheless, he had no intention of letting her get away from him this morning and if she thought to knock him off his game by throwing him out, then she'd better think again. Payne gathered his things and sidled over to the door, where she was waiting for him. Rather than stating the obvious— that making love to her had been beyond amazing—he lowered his head and brushed a kiss on her forehead. "Enemies again?" he asked.

"Opponents," Emma clarified, her voice oddly strangled. "We're opponents."

Semantics, he supposed, but he preferred her term to his as well. Enemies suggested that they had nothing in common, that they couldn't get along. They'd proven without a doubt last night that they not only could get along, but they could do it splendidly.

Payne nodded and walked out into the hall. "I'll see you at breakfast."

Her gaze tangled with his and a small smile played over her lips. "Don't count on it." And with that parting shot, she closed the door.

Oh, but he would, Payne thought. She wouldn't get out of here this morning before he was damned good and ready for her to go. Just because he normally didn't break the rules didn't mean he was opposed to bending them himself when the need arose.

And now would be a good time for her to learn that.

11

"THAT SNEAKY BASTARD," Emma muttered, staring at Payne's Bug.

Last night it had been parked beside her Hummer—this morning it was parked *behind* it.

Unless she wanted to back over it—which was heartily tempting—she had no way of getting out of the parking lot, much less getting away from him. She resisted the childish urge to stamp her foot and swallowed the frustrated scream that automatically rose in her throat.

She should have anticipated something like this, but frankly, she wouldn't have thought that he'd stoop to such a sneaky, underhanded crafty trick. It was more *her* style, she thought, reluctantly impressed.

When had he done this? she wondered, glaring at the car as though she could move it with the force of her gaze. Certainly it couldn't have been last night—he'd been with her. Her body did a little meltdown, remembering. Before dinner then? She didn't think so. Someone would have noticed and said something about it. No, it had to have been this morning.

Then it hit her.

He must have turned on his shower, then left it running while he sneaked downstairs and moved the car. She hadn't heard the motor start, but then she doubted that she would have, because she hadn't been listening for it. She'd been too busy scurrying around, trying to finish getting ready to pay attention to any noise other than his shower, which she'd noted had taken an especially long time. In fact, it had still been running when she'd hurried downstairs. In retrospect, that should have tipped her off. Payne was too efficient to linger in the shower.

Before completely giving up, she checked the doors to the vehicle and swore when she found them both locked. If he hadn't locked them, she could have popped it out of gear and rolled the damned thing out of her way. As it was, she was stuck.

And she was fuming.

Muttering a string of curse words which would

have made her mother head for a bar of soap, Emma strode back into the house. She made an unnecessary trip upstairs to look for Payne in his room, then backtracked downstairs once more and found him in the dining room.

His hair still damp, he looked up at her and smiled as she stomped toward his table. "You're joining me for breakfast?"

"No. I'm joining you at your car. Come move it," she ground out.

Looking slightly smug, Payne calmly slathered butter over his hotcakes. "I will when I'm ready to leave."

"Do it *now*."

"You should really try some of these," he said, ignoring her order. "They're fabulous. I missed breakfast yesterday," he remarked casually, though there was an edge to his voice that made her skin prickle.

An implied "because of you" hung between them.

Emma felt her cheeks pinken. "Could you please just move your damned car?" she pleaded. "I have things to do."

Payne looked up and his cool gaze tangled with hers. "I know that," he explained patiently, "because we're doing the same thing. I thought today we should go together."

Emma felt her jaw drop. "Go together? Have you lost your mind?"

He selected a piece of bacon. "It saves me the time of having to find you."

She crossed her arms over her chest and chewed the inside of her cheek to keep from screaming. "Here's a thought," she said, practically firing the words at him. "Why don't you stop trying to find me and start looking for the damned pocketwatch," she said shrilly.

This was completely counterproductive, and definitely not part of her plan, but for some reason she'd lost sight of that. It was probably because now, if he was near her, she knew she'd want to have sex with him. And, after last night, she grimly suspected she wouldn't be choosy about *where*. The Hummer, the Bug, the antique malls, the side of the building. It didn't matter. He had that kind of effect on her. She became mindless and stupid and desperate and the thought of having that big, hard body of his pumping in and out of hers made her belly and thighs clench and her sex tingle and slicken.

"Why don't you sit down and have some breakfast?" Payne countered. "It's the most important meal of the day."

"I'm not here for a lecture on nutrition, Payne," she snapped. "I'm here to find that pocketwatch before you do. Just because we had sex last night doesn't mean that anything has changed."

"I figured that out when you threw me out this morning," he drawled, shooting her a cool look. "But for the record, I never expected it to."

Emma inwardly squirmed, not altogether proud of herself for waking him up and sending him on his way. Brian Payne awake was formidable and thrilling—Brian Payne asleep and vulnerable was somehow more so.

Emma had stood next to the bed and traced the beautiful landscape of his face, the straight line of his nose, the angled curve of his jaw and those amazingly perfect lips. She'd been strangely awed by the soft patch of skin next to his eyes, the soft, sweet curl of the little hairs behind his ears. Her stomach had felt queasy and a weird pang had squeezed her chest, one that was almost too intense to bear because it smacked of a tender emotion which had no business between them.

That's when she'd poked him.

She'd had to, or she would have crawled back

into that bed with him and they would have made love again. And then they would have slept until noon and possibly never left the room. And as fantastic as that would have been, it wouldn't have put her any closer to finding the pocketwatch and securing her future.

Only an idiot would want to nurse a bud of romance between her and Brian Payne, knowing that the inevitable first frost of the relationship would leave her brokenhearted, broke and wretched. And Emma was many things, but an idiot wasn't one of them. So, though she'd winced inside, she'd woken him up and shown him to the door, firmly convinced that all would go according to her plan.

That part had been wrong, she thought, smiling up at Harry as he slid a stack of hotcakes and sausage in front of her. But the day wasn't over yet and she still had a few tricks up her sleeve.

He might have won this battle, but he hadn't yet won the war.

"Fine," Emma relented, as though she actually had a choice. "I'll wait on you to move your car."

"How about you ride with me today?"

"Sorry," she said sweetly. "I'm claustrophobic."

"Then I'll ride with you."

No, he wouldn't, Emma thought, but didn't say anything. She could argue with him, but that would only turn her on, and then she might actually relent. Better to let him think he held the upper hand, then show him otherwise later.

After breakfast, Payne made a point to go and tell Matthew how much he enjoyed it before walking outside where she'd been waiting on him. She climbed into the Hummer and let it warm up while he descended the steps.

"I'll be right back," he told her as he opened the door to the Bug.

Making a point to look stoically resigned to his presence, Emma merely nodded. The instant he moved the car, however, she put the Hummer in gear and spun gravel, shooting out of the driveway. Payne's thunderous expression filled her rearview mirror, making a long peel of laughter bubble up in her throat. She powered the window down and twinkled her fingers at him as she drove away without him.

He followed her, of course, but the priceless look on his face was worth her petty act of defiance. Just because he was used to giving orders didn't mean she had to take them.

The sooner he learned that, the better off he'd be.

"YOU'RE A PIECE OF WORK, you know that?" Payne remarked. He leaned against the building she was about to go into, but didn't follow her.

"I try," she said. With her hand poised on the doorknob, she frowned at him. "What? Do you have some sort of psychic way of knowing that the pocketwatch isn't in this store?"

He dumped a package of peanuts down his throat and chased it with a drink of soda. "No."

She cocked her head, seemingly exasperated. "Then why aren't you following me?"

"I thought you didn't want me to follow you."

Emma looked heavenward, releasing a small put-upon sigh. "That hasn't stopped you in the past. So why aren't you following me now?"

"Because I went into that particular shop yesterday while I was looking for you and I already know that it's not there."

She blinked at him, annoyed. "Then why the hell did you let me drive over here?"

"I would have stopped you if I'd been in the car with you," Payne told her.

Her eyes widened. "You're still pouting because I left you?"

"I'm not pouting," Payne said through suddenly clenched teeth. He didn't pout, dammit. "I'm just saying that since we're both looking for the same thing, it would go a whole lot faster if we'd simply combine the search." And, yes, it had been particularly maddening when she'd driven off without him, but given what he'd witnessed over the past few days, he didn't know why he'd been surprised. She'd merely been acting in character.

He was the one who'd slipped out of it.

"Then what happens when we both find it, Captain Logic?" she asked, smiling as though he were an imbecile. "Are we going to build a fire and sing 'Kumbaya'?"

"Whoever puts their hand on it first gets it," Payne told her.

And he fully intended to let her find it first, then buy it from her for Hastings's price. Emma wanted to complete the mission—to best him—and get the money. She could have all three and he could fulfill his favor for Garrett.

He would have his freedom, Emma would have her new start, and if it cost him a little cash, then so be it. He inwardly shrugged. It's not like he didn't have the money, and in this case, he didn't mind spending it. A telling truth lay in that insight, but Payne didn't care to explore it.

Instead, he studied Emma and tried to gauge her thoughts.

Several beats passed while she weighed her decision. "Let me think about it," she finally told him. She grimaced. "Right now I need to find a little girl's room."

He nodded, pleased that she hadn't discounted the idea outright. He'd fully expected her to, but clearly she recognized that she was spending too much time trying to avoid him and not enough time looking for the watch. That was progress, Payne thought, settling in outside the store to wait for her.

Ten minutes later, cursing hotly under his breath, he realized he'd been had. He strolled around the store, looking for her and when the search came up empty, resigned himself to asking the clerk where she'd gone.

"She asked to use the bathroom. I don't know where she went after that."

"Is there a back door?"

"There is, but she couldn't have gone out that way. We're unloading a truck right now, and it's backed flush against the door."

Then she had to have come out the front door, right past him. As implausible as it seemed, she'd somehow managed to walk right by him without him realizing it. This was freaking unbelievable, Payne thought, as he stalked out of the shop. A stabbing pain developed behind his right eye and he was suddenly hit with the insane urge to lean his head back and howl. How in God's name had he allowed this woman to get so far under his skin that he couldn't even keep track of her? He'd tailed terrorists with better success, dammit.

Payne paused outside the door, forced himself to concentrate. Who'd come out? he wondered. He thought back. A man, mid-forties with a balding pate. An older lady who'd walked with a cane and a younger petite blonde. That'd been it. Emma hadn't—

A younger petite blonde...

A wig, Payne realized. She hadn't needed to pee—the ruthless witch had needed to go get into disguise. Payne stood there, astonished. A slow disbelieving smile spread across his lips and, if he hadn't been so damned annoyed, he'd be impressed. Ruthless and resourceful. With his luck, she was going to find the pocketwatch before he did and then she'd disappear without so much as a backward glance.

For some reason, the idea of never seeing her again was a lot more distressing than losing this infernal contest. He frowned, forcing the thought from his mind.

At any rate, his plan was crucial to him finding it first. He was trying to do the right thing, dammit, trying to be noble. And she was thwarting him at every opportunity.

Actually, a little voice spoke up, the noble thing to do would be to bow out completely, but for whatever reason, Payne simply couldn't do it. The idea of losing was so foreign to him, he couldn't even entertain it. Furthermore, the favor would only be fulfilled if he won—if he delivered the pocketwatch to Garrett. Freedom lay in *that* plan and God knows he needed it. In fact, he needed that freedom from obligation as much as Emma Langsford needed Hastings's money.

Would she see it that way? Payne paused, consideringly. To be fair, yes, she probably would. But that wouldn't stop her from trying to complete her task any more than knowing she needed the money was making him give up his.

His lips twisted. He supposed that made him every bit as ruthless as she was.

Determined to find her once again, Payne made his way back to where they'd parked and breathed a silent sigh of relief that the H2 was still there.

Knowing where she'd been helped narrow things down, so rather than take off on a fool's errand, Payne put his pragmatic mind to work and determined that she had to be one of three places.

Naturally, he found her in the third. His lips quirked as he watched her blow the long blond hair out of her face while she pored over another display case. He noticed that she'd changed sweaters as well. This morning she'd worn a pale green cable-knit—now she sported an Ole Miss sweatshirt.

Heat detonated in his loins as he watched her and he was suddenly hit with how arousing this little cat and mouse game between them had been. Aside from being annoying, it was damned fun. She was a worthy adversary, an equal, he realized with a start, wondering if he'd ever met a female counterpart before. He instinctively knew he hadn't.

Payne spotted a bathroom in the back and calculated the time it would take to get her in there. He quietly stole up behind her, slid his fingers against the back of her neck and heard her gasp. The sound made his dick jerk hard against his jeans.

"Another point for you," he said silkily, glad

that he'd taken the time to hit a drugstore before finding her. "Want to claim your prize?"

Emma turned around. Her gaze was guarded, but dark with a desire he knew matched his own. "What's that?"

"Me," he said, bending down and sliding his tongue over her bottom lip.

She whimpered, torn. *"Payne."*

"You know you want me."

He threaded his fingers through hers and tugged her toward the bathroom. The second the door closed behind them, he flipped the lock, tugged the wig off and went for the snap at his jeans. She shucked her own, not bothering with her shirt. A second later, he sheathed himself in a condom, picked her up and backed her against the wall.

Half a second later he was inside of her and his world brightened immensely.

She laughed, seemingly as relieved as he felt to be holding her, taking her. "Oh, God, Payne. This is crazy." She nipped at his neck.

He pumped harder, back and forth, back and forth, letting a newer, better tension take hold. "I can't help it," he confessed. "When I see you, some-thing inside of me snaps and I've got to have you."

She kissed him, pulling his tongue deep into her mouth and sucking it, mimicking the blow job she'd given him last night. He felt his legs weaken as the beginnings of climax gathered force in his loins.

"I know what you mean," she said. "I've been thinking about licking you all over since I ran into you at the airport." He felt her clench her feminine muscles around him, holding on to him. "You're big and strong and so damned calm I want to shake you up, to *make* you lose it," she growled.

She certainly had a way of doing that, he thought. He pounded into her greedy body, pushed and pushed until he was certain someone was going to hear them. But he didn't give a damn. She was hot and tiny and for the moment, his, and he wanted nothing more than to lose himself inside of her.

Emma pumped and flexed harder against him and he knew she was close, knew that the same madness that was pounding through his veins had entered hers, as well. Her body suddenly went rigid and she clamped around him over and over again, triggering his own orgasm.

It blasted from his loins with enough force to blow the end out the condom, but at the moment he didn't give a damn. He locked his knees to keep them from giving way and held her around him while the last contractions of her own release milked his.

Breathing hard, he kissed her cheek and settled his forehead against hers. "God, woman, you're going to be the death of me. Don't hide from me again," he told her, meaning it in more ways than he should. "It's insulting."

_12_

"YOU KNOW, I'm starting to wonder if the damn thing even exists."

"The pocketwatch?" Payne asked.

Emma nodded, scooping up a handful of grain and letting the strawberry roan nibble from her palm. Dubbed Cinnamon, Emma and the horse had become fast friends over the past couple of days.

Much like she and Payne, she thought, a soft smile curling her lips.

"I've wondered that myself," he said. Looking oddly in his element, he was currently stroking Lazarus, the dappled gray Harry had told them he'd saved from the slaughterhouse.

Ever since the bathroom incident, when Payne had told her to stop hiding from him, Emma had given up trying to give him the slip. There'd been a desperate, almost vulnerable quality to his order that had made something in her heart stir and, while she firmly intended to get to the pocket-watch before him—even if it meant she had to wrestle him for it—she fully believed that he was a man of his word. He'd said whoever put their hand on it first won. She mentally shrugged.

Simple enough.

It was a waste of both of their time to duplicate efforts and, since they'd combined forces over the past couple of days, they'd covered considerably more ground. They'd canvassed every antique and hole-in-the-wall shop in the area, had cross-referenced the owners of said shops with the names on the list which had been provided by the auction house, thereby ruling out a few of those so-called leads.

Today they'd interviewed half a dozen people who'd bought watches from that auction and planned to talk to the others tomorrow. After that, they'd have exhausted every lead and would either have to concede defeat—a prospect she didn't even want to entertain—or start again from scratch.

Emma knew from Norah that Payne had only booked himself into The Dove's Nest through Friday. A quick peek at his plane ticket last night when they'd stopped by his room for another condom had confirmed an early Saturday morning return flight to Atlanta. He'd turned his back to take a call and the ticket had been lying on the dresser in plain sight, so technically she hadn't been snooping. She'd merely been curious.

At any rate, the same sick feeling she'd experienced when she'd discovered that little tidbit had returned every time she'd thought about it since. Even now her stomach churned with dread and angst, a miserable cocktail which could only mean guaranteed heartache when this week was over.

Though he hadn't spent the whole night with her—a result of her none-to-gentle approach to waking him up and throwing him out the first time, she imagined—she and Payne had spent practically every minute together since. They'd fallen into a smooth rhythm of sex, meals, good conversation and searching for the pocketwatch, which had come so easily to them that it was downright eerie. And with every second spent in his company, Emma could feel herself losing ground, fighting on a slippery slope she had no business being on in the first place.

Bu Payne was…fascinating.

He was not just smart, but *brilliant*. Factor in

his extreme sense of honor, that almost unshakable facade, his substantial sex appeal and a twisted sense of humor only a girl with an equally twisted sense of humor could appreciate and you had the recipe for the perfect man.

Or at least he would be if he wanted to be any woman's perfect man.

Which he clearly didn't.

Emma knew that she got to him on a physical level. Aside from him routinely dragging her into bed—or the nearest bathroom as the case may be—she could tell that this "thing" they had was out of the realm of his experience, too. She couldn't walk near him that he didn't touch her— a brush of his fingers over the back of her neck, his hand at her elbow or his fingers tangled in hers.

Furthermore, given the odd little looks he gave her, she knew that something was at work in that practical mind of his. She got the impression that he didn't know quite what to make of her, that he was trying to put her in a neat little category, but couldn't find one that fit. She'd watched flashes of respect, admiration, desire and exasperation light up those cool wintry eyes and she'd be lying if she said they didn't affect her. Emma let go a shuddering breath.

Brian Payne affected her on a molecular level.

She could feel him in her very blood, in her bones, knew instinctively when he was near. The mere sound of his voice made a thrill of warm joy bolt through her, one that made her throat go tight and her heart melt with ever-growing affection.

Was she in love with him? Not yet…but if she didn't find that pocketwatch and get away from him soon, then no doubt she would be.

And no amount of self-preservation would save her.

Payne sidled closer to her, slinging an arm around her shoulder and offering a smile. "Getting cold?" he asked.

Emma shook her head. "Not really. You throw off heat like a blast furnace, so I can always snuggle up next to you."

"Why don't we go back upstairs and you can *snuggle* on top of me?"

Emma chuckled as a dart of heat landed squarely in her womb. "I'm beginning to think you're addicted to sex."

"Funny," he said, drawing her closer. "I'm beginning to think I'm addicted to you."

Unexpected delight bloomed in her chest. She turned and grinned up at him. "I'm a hard habit to break," she teased. "But no worries. Come Saturday you'll get to quit me, cold turkey."

A flicker of something—regret, maybe?—danced in his eyes, but it was gone so fast Emma was inclined to believe that she'd imagined it. He quirked a brow. "What happens Saturday?"

She swallowed a disappointed sigh. "You go back to Atlanta. I saw your plane ticket," she confessed. Not sheepishly, though. That wasn't her style.

He inclined his head, continued to study her. "What about you? When are you going back?"

"I've got an open-ended ticket, but I imagine Hastings will call me home when you leave. I think he wanted to win the bet more than he wanted the pocketwatch." She shrugged, trying to appear unconcerned. "Once you exit the scene, the bet's over."

He gave her one of those long unreadable looks, the kind that made her feel like he was peering directly into her head. "Maybe we'll find it before then," he said, not offering to stay longer.

She hadn't expected him to, of course. He had a life and a business to go back to—one that he evidently enjoyed. It wasn't his fault that her life sucked and that she wasn't equally anxious to return to Marble Springs. All she had waiting for her was more work for less pay and a longer sentence at the Hefty Hog.

Nevertheless, she'd banked ten grand which would take care of the taxes and catch up the mortgage. School would be a little longer in coming, but not as long as it would have been without Hastings's errand, so she was more thankful than disappointed. Still, she thought, casting a wistful glance at Cinnamon and Lazarus, it would have been nice to jump right into school. Now that she'd finally figured out what she wanted to do, she couldn't wait to get about the business of doing it.

"We've still got several people to see tomorrow," Payne said, carefully studying her. "You know what they say. You always find what you're seeking in the last place that you look."

Emma couldn't help it—she grinned. "Well, of course you do, you big nimrod," she said. "Why the hell would you keep looking for something if you've already found it?"

He smiled down at her, bent and kissed the end of her nose. "You're adorable, you know that?"

"I prefer 'adorable' to 'smart-ass,'" she told him, citing the name he'd been calling her last night.

His head tilted to a thoughtful angle. "Actually 'adorable smart-ass' fits perfectly."

Better than being an unadorable dumb-ass, she supposed. "We should probably head back up to the house," she remarked. "Matthew will have dinner ready soon."

Payne nodded. "Why don't we get a movie from the library afterward?"

He wanted to watch a movie with her as opposed to having sex the instant they went back upstairs? Like a date? Emma thought as a balloon of happiness expanded in her chest. "Sure," she said, unreasonably pleased.

He nodded, laced his fingers through hers and tugged her toward the house. "Any preferences?"

"I'm not picky," she confessed. A thought occurred. She shot him a sidelong look and qualified her comment. "Just no porn."

Payne's deep chuckle vibrated off her spine, sending little tingles of pleasure curling through her. It was deep, sexy, intimate laugh, the kind between lovers. "No worries. I'm not into *watching* it as much as I'm into *making* it."

"I'D LOVE TO GET A PEEK at one of those ghosts, wouldn't you?" Emma asked as they waited their turn to thank Judith and Matilda, the cross-dressing pig, for a night of ghost story hogwash, er, entertainment, Payne amended. Honestly, he fell strictly into the seeing-is-believing camp in this instance. Not that he didn't have faith, but this… This was just too much.

Judith had spun several tales involving both Confederate and Union soldiers which had reportedly been spotted in and around The Dove's Nest. Evidently the Inn had been used as a Confederate hospital after the battle of Gettysburg and, according to Harry and Norah, they'd both seen the ghost of who they believed was a Private Jeremy Roberts. Jeremy and his three younger brothers had all lost their lives at Pickett's Charge and Jeremy still wandered the halls of The Dove's Nest today, looking for his fallen brothers.

Payne couldn't deny that he'd had a bit of a weird feeling when he and Emma had toured the battlefield today. He believed that too much death and destruction—thousands upon thousands of lives lost—had somehow imprinted its pain into the very ground. Fanciful? Maybe. But that kind of loss commanded respect—reverence—and as such, he and Emma had both appreciated the eerie silence as they'd walked through the battlefield.

But ghosts? He supposed it was possible, but until he came face to face with one, he'd undoubtedly remain a skeptic. Payne frowned.

Just like he was skeptical that Robert E. Lee's pocketwatch actually existed. Emma had made the comment a couple of days ago about that very thing and, knowing what finding it had meant to her, he'd kept his own counsel.

But after almost a week-long search with no luck and no possibility of luck, Payne grimly suspected that the pocketwatch tale was simply a story, much like the ones they'd heard here tonight.

Though she'd kept a stiff upper lip this afternoon when they'd left their last possible lead, Payne knew that she'd been privately disappointed. Her slim shoulders had rounded with uncharacteristic defeat and she'd stared out the window, watching the passing landscape, lost in her own thoughts. Given the resigned look on her face, they hadn't been happy ones.

For whatever reason, that look had been practically unbearable, and he'd been hit with the almost inexplicable urge to make things right for her. To help her. He'd considered offering her a job, hell giving her the money himself—an indication that he had lost any grasp on his former reality—but he knew that she wouldn't be interested in either. Emma wanted to make her own way and anything that smacked of a handout would undoubtedly result in him getting smacked back. The thought drew a smile.

One way or another, though, he'd find a way to help her.

Unfortunately, time had run out in this instance and his legendary brain had yet to produce an answer to his very immediate problem.

Payne supposed he could change his ticket and stay for the rest of the weekend, but after careful thought—and no small amount of cowardice—he'd decided that he needed to leave in the morning, if for no other reason than to prove to himself that he could. Every instinct tugged at him to stay—to be with her—but old fears had reared their ugly heads, polluting his thinking. The idea that Emma could influence him beyond good sense did more than simply alarm him—it terrified him.

He needed some distance to pull his thoughts together, to come up with a new way to help her, and for whatever reason, it had become imperative that he do that at home. Did he care about her?

Payne's throat clogged with some nebulous obstruction and he swallowed a bark of dry laughter.

More than he wanted to.

More than he would admit.

More than he ever dreamed possible.

But he *would not* become a slave to emotion any more than he would allow her to lead him around like a bear with a ring in its nose. He would not—no matter how much he cared about her—allow her to make a fool of him.

He would not be like his father.

"Judith, that was fantastic," Emma said. "Very entertaining."

At last, Payne thought with a silent sigh. Their turn. Then they could go up to bed and get started on creating a proper last night together. One that involved naked skin, hot sighs, hotter sex and bone-tingling orgasms.

Judith smiled warmly. "I'm glad that you enjoyed yourself, dear."

Her lips curled in a wobbly grin, Emma gestured toward Matilda. "Er…what's with the tuxedo and top hat?"

Judith rolled her eyes. "Gender identity crisis," she said in a stage whisper, as though the pig could hear or understand her. "Doc Newton assures me this is just a phase, but I can't do anything with her. She refuses to wear any of the new dresses I've made for her and pitched a snorting fit when I tried to put a necklace around her neck." She cast an exasperated glance at Matilda. "Ornery hog."

Emma pressed a hand to her mouth to stifle a giggle and Payne had to bite his tongue to keep from saying something completely inappropriate. Like, *She's a pig! What the hell are you doing putting clothes on her in the first place?*

Payne's gaze dropped to Matilda and he barely smothered a snort. She wore a top hat and tuxedo, complete with a red satin cummerbund. And Matilda might have balked at wearing a necklace, but that hadn't stopped Judith from attaching a pocketwatch to the hog's chest.

…a pocketwatch to the hog's chest.

Payne stilled and every sense went on point. No, he thought, staring at the gold watch glinting from the front of the tuxedo. It couldn't be. Not after everything they had been through this week. It was too simple. What sort of twist of fate would put Robert E. Lee's father's timepiece on a spoiled cross-dressing potbellied pig? It was unfathom—

Emma tugged at his hand. "You ready?"

Payne's gaze swung to hers and he forced

himself into lockdown mode. "Actually, I wanted a minute with Matthew. You want to go on up and I'll meet you?" Payne knew she would assume that he wanted to compliment the cook—he'd been making a point to do that after each meal—and, at the moment, he was content to let her think that.

Emma nodded. "Sure. I'll see you in a few minutes then."

He waited until Emma mounted the stairs, then quickly turned to Judith. "That's a nice pocketwatch Matilda's wearing," he remarked casually. "Where did you get it?"

"Oh, that old piece of junk?" Judith laughed. "I got it from an estate sale a few months ago."

Anticipation spiked as the implication of what she'd just said sunk in. Granted Judith's name hadn't been on either one of their lists, but Garrett had said it had been a slipshod job. It could have easily happened. "Do you mind if I take a look at it?" Payne asked.

Judith shrugged. "Sure. Suit yourself." She bent down and retrieved the watch from Matilda's chest, then handed it to Payne.

Though his blood was brimming with adrenaline, Payne's hands were steady, his face impassive as he inspected the timepiece. He studied the front, knew from the brand it was the right time period, then casually turned it over, looking for the inscription.

And there it was—*Lighthorse.*

He chuckled softly and shook his head. Well, I'll be damned, he thought. After everything they had been through the past week, the damned watch had been added to the wardrobe of a pig the entire time. He was certain that stranger things had happened, but he sure as hell couldn't think of anything at the moment.

"If you like it, you can keep it," Judith said. "Matilda has plenty of other accessories."

"Let me pay you for it," Payne told her, uncomfortable with the gift.

"No, no," Judith insisted. She closed his fingers around it and squeezed. "Consider it a keepsake from your time here at The Dove's Nest."

"Thank you," he said. "I appreciate it." More than you will ever know, he silently added.

He slipped the watch into his pants pocket, vastly relieved that Emma wouldn't go home empty-handed. He couldn't give it to her of course— she'd never accept it—but instead would have to set the stage for her to find it herself. This would mean enlisting help—Norah, the romantic, he decided, knowing that this would be right up her alley. And he'd have to stay for one more day. Once Emma put her hand on it first—translate, beat him, the competitive little wench—then he could make her a better offer. She'd take it, because she was smart and needed the money, and then he could hand it over to Garrett.

End of favor.

Debt paid.

Payne expelled a heavy breath. It was a round-about, convoluted ridiculous way to meet his ends, particularly when he'd just pocketed the freedom he'd been desperately seeking for the past several months, but knowing how much Emma needed it, as well… Payne just couldn't do it.

The last thing he ever expected to do was help a woman with money problems—after all, that very type of woman had been the bane of his father's existence—but then again, he'd never met a more hardworking determined woman than Emma Langsford, either.

She was…*it*.

The profoundness of that thought made him pause right outside her door and he grew completely still, momentarily unable to move. He waited for a clap of thunder to rent the heavens, a bolt of lightning—anything that would announce the gravity of what he'd just realized—but, strangely, nothing happened. Instead a quiet peace stole over him, followed by a slow dawning smile.

Then he opened her door and walked into heaven.

_13_

PAYNE'S NEED TO TIP Matthew in compliments as opposed to cash had actually worked out in Emma's favor. She'd taken a few minutes to sexy herself up, to slip on the least unattractive gown she'd brought with her, a vintage nylon Grecian gown her mother had found for her at a bargain store. It was an icy green with hundreds of tiny accordion pleats and it never failed to make her feel like a forties-era Hollywood starlet. Deciding on candles, she'd turned off every light with the exception of the sconces on either side of the fireplace and, as a result, the room glowed with a cozy warmth.

This was her last night with Payne—a lump formed in her throat at the thought, but she determinedly swallowed it—and, as such, she wanted this final evening to be special.

She wanted him to know that _he_ was special. To her.

Emma wasn't exactly sure when it had

happened, but over the past few days, Brian Payne had become increasingly important to her. In the morning he would get on a plane and go back to Atlanta, and she firmly believed that she'd most likely never hear from him again. She'd go home and tell herself that this week had been a once-in-a-lifetime romantic fluke and that these intense feelings she had for him would subside and fade, right along with the memories they'd made together.

She would tell herself that…and hoped like hell she became a better liar than she was at present.

Wishful thinking on all of the above, but what the hell. Her lips curled into a rueful smile. If she was going to delude herself, she might as well do it big.

Payne chose that moment to walk into her room. He didn't bother to knock, because he knew he didn't have to. He knew he was welcome. Into her room, into her body. Not necessarily into her heart, but that, she'd just come to realize, was a foregone conclusion, one she didn't have any control over. She imagined she'd have just as much luck evicting him from her heart as she would making it stop beating. And since suicide was out of the question, she'd simply have to learn to deal with it.

Payne's cool gaze started at her feet and was a scorching blue flame by the time it tangled with hers. While another man might have made a compliment, he didn't bother. He didn't have to. She'd read everything in his gaze and it was a lot more thrilling than any token remark he might have made. A man of action, he strolled across the room, tilted her chin up and very deliberately kissed the strength right out of her backbone. Emma's senses instantly caught fire and she sagged against him, offering her lips up for his taking.

All week long he'd been desperate, hurried, seemingly unable to help himself when it came to being with her. He'd been *driven,* for lack of a better explanation. But tonight he was different. Tonight, there was a reverence in his still-hungry touch that made the backs of her lids burn, an unspoken emotion boiling under the surface of this particular siege.

Emma allowed him to set the pace, fell into his rhythm. He kissed and suckled, rubbed and kneaded, slowly slipped her gown off her shoulders, then stood back and admired her as it fell into a satiny puddle around her feet.

"God, you're beautiful," Payne told her, his voice oddly thick.

Emma smiled. She certainly felt that way when he looked at her like that. Like she was dipped in chocolate, rolled in icing, covered in sprinkles with a cherry on top and he hadn't had a good sundae in…*never.* A warm flutter winged through her belly, making her breath catch in her throat.

"Thank you," Emma finally said. She stepped forward, slowly unbuttoned his shirt and slid her palms over the wide expanse of his chest. *Supple skin, firm muscle…masculine perfection.* "You're pretty damned beautiful yourself," she said, feeling her lids flutter beneath the weight of delicious sensation. Touching him made her drunk with longing, made her want to wrap her legs around his waist and sink onto his sex—the ultimate fix.

As though he'd read her thoughts again, Payne's gaze burned even hotter. He shrugged out of his shirt and shucked his pants and boxers, kicking them aside. His dick jutted proudly forward, huge and mouthwatering, just like the rest of him. He nudged her backward toward the bed, kissing her all the while. Emma felt the cool quilt at her back and a hot man on top of her and the sensation was…indescribable. Her womb contracted, coating her folds and a hot, insistent buzz beat upon her clit, making her squirm toward that part of him she so desperately needed.

Murmuring masculine sounds of pleasure, Payne kissed and licked his way down her body. Her neck, her breasts, a long deliberate trail down her abdomen, stopping only long enough to sample her bellybutton. Then he parted her curls and blew a steady stream of hot air against her weeping flesh.

Emma opened wider for him, shamelessly baring herself to him. He dragged a finger down her folds, dipped deeply inside, gathering even more juices, then painted her outer folds and aching clit with them. She bit her lip and squirmed beneath his ministrations, felt her stomach tremble as he dabbled and played. Then, without warning, he fastened his mouth upon her and she arched up off the bed, so intense was the sensation.

He sucked hard, slipped a finger deep inside of her and hooked it around, locating a patch of super-sensitive skin she hadn't known existed. He worked his tongue against her clit, massaged her inside until Emma thought for sure she would pass out from the pure joy bolting through her. She writhed beneath him, knew that release was coming and when it did, would come *hard*.

Just when she was certain he couldn't do anything more to please her, anything more to surprise her, he pressed a knuckle against the rosebud of her bottom and half a second later her world shattered.

She came violently, so forcefully that she skated the fringes of passing out completely. Her head thrashed from side to side, her back arched away from the bed and she fisted her hands in the quilt, hanging on to consciousness as a silent yawning scream of release tore from her throat.

Sweet God, Emma thought, then *Save me,* as Payne suddenly loomed between her legs—his gaze, intent and desperate and filled with some sort of hidden meaning she couldn't understand, bored into hers—and then thrust deeply inside of her. She came again, this time harder than the first. It was savage yet tender and her silly heart melted right along with the rest of her body.

Payne paused, seemed to be making sure she could take the rest of what was to come. Utterly drained but strangely energized, Emma smiled faintly and flexed her feminine muscles around him, drawing him deeper into her body. "Don't stop," she said, breathing heavily. "It's insulting."

PAYNE PLUNGED BACK INSIDE her greedy little body, felt her legs wrap around his waist, her heels dig into his ass, urging him on, and raced as hard and as fast as he could toward release.

He could still taste her on his lips, could have fed between her thighs all night. She'd been warm and sweet and wet and delicious and he'd been damned lucky he hadn't come when he'd tasted her.

He'd wanted things to be different tonight, to show that he more than desired her—that he needed her—but somewhere past the first kiss, the first brush of her hands across his chest, he'd lost sight of that goal because his senses had been clouded by another. He'd wanted to be tender, to be gentle, to make love to her in that cool, methodical way that he'd painstakingly perfected, that he'd built his reputation on.

Unfortunately, he couldn't.

One taste of her, one touch from her and he became an animal, unable to control even the most basic urges. Payne knew there was nothing gentle in the way he was taking her—he'd screwed her halfway across the bed already and if he didn't back off, he'd undoubtedly screw her right off the mattress, but he couldn't seem to help himself. Instead, he seemed to be determined to take her so hard and so completely that the idea of ever making love to another man would get jarred right out of her stubborn little head.

Later, when the blood returned to his brain, he would realize that this probably wasn't the best course of action—in fact, that it made absolutely no sense.

But for the moment, while she was tightening around him, biting at his shoulder, clawing, screaming, grunting and groaning from his brutal bedding, it made perfect, logical sense.

He could feel release spinning like a tornado in the back of his balls, preparing to sweep down the length of his aching dick and erupt into her and the idea that his seed was about to flood her womb—that he'd been so caught up in having her that he hadn't taken precaution—was such a friggin' turn-on, he dug his toes into the mattress, angled deeper and came hard. He should have been scared, terrified, and yet he wasn't.

A long, keening groan tore from his throat and

his back spasmed from the force of the climax. When the last contractions pulsed through him, Payne carefully withdrew, then rolled onto the mattress next to her and pulled her to him.

Breathing heavily, limp as a dishrag all over, he pressed a kiss at her temple. "I don't want this to be over, Emma," he said, laying it all on the line.

She turned and looked up at him. "Who said it has to be?" She paused, ran a hand over his chest. "My tub's big enough for two. Wanna share a bubble bath?"

Utterly spent, Payne chuckled softly. "That's all I could share at the moment."

Emma disentangled herself from him and started toward the bathroom. She shot him a droll look over her shoulder. "Don't get up. I'll do it."

"What?" he asked innocently. "Did you need my help?"

He must have drifted off to sleep because when he next awoke—it couldn't have been more than a few minutes; he could still hear the water running into the tub from the bathroom—Emma was standing next to the bed, her face a white mask of pain and anger. Payne blinked, pulling her into focus.

And that's when he saw it.

The pocketwatch dangled from the chain around her fingers and spun slowly, much like the alarm suddenly swirling in his belly.

"When did you find this?" she asked, her voice ominously controlled, completely out of character.

"Tonight," Payne answered truthfully. He sat up, glanced at his pants lying in the floor and a horrible suspicion took hold. "Did you go through my pockets?"

Had she been doing that all along? Payne suddenly wondered. Had she been using him? Staying close to him so that if he did find the pocketwatch before her, she could take it from him? Granted in the beginning he'd used much the same strategy, but he would never have taken it from her.

Watch your back, man, Guy had said. *Sounds like this chick is capable of putting a knife in it.*

Oh, no, Payne thought, mentally shaking his head. This could not be happening. He could not have allowed himself to be hoodwinked by this slip of a woman. He could not have allowed himself to get knocked so far off his game—to be such a bad judge of character—that she had completely pulled the wool over his eyes and made a fool of him. He set his jaw so hard he feared it would crack and an image of his drunken, miserable father loomed large in his mind.

Emma studied him for a long moment, then her lips formed a smirk and she shook her head. "Wondering if I'm that ruthless, Payne?" she asked, once again using that uncanny ability of peering into his head. "Wondering if you've misjudged me? Don't," she said. "It's insulting."

She dropped the pocketwatch into his lap, then marched to her door and opened it. "Get out."

"Emma—"

She glared at him with so much hatred he felt himself flinch, and in that instant he realized he'd made a terrible mistake. *"Get out,"* she repeated.

And she meant more than out of this room— she was kicking him out of her life, as well. Panic made his throat tighten and his stomach sour.

Rather than provoke her further, he silently gathered his things, then paused at the door. "Emma, let me explain. Look, I'm sor—"

"Save it," she said, her gaze trained on the hardwood floor beneath her bare feet. "Goodbye, Major Payne."

She gave him a none-too-gentle shove past the threshold, then quietly closed the door. Unfortunately it wasn't thick enough to disguise the soft thud of her forehead hitting it, or the quiet sobs he could hear from the other side.

Payne squeezed the pocketwatch so hard he felt it cut into his palm. His chest ached and the urge to go right back in there to her and apologize until she had to believe him was almost overpowering. Unfortunately, if he'd learned anything about Emma Langsford over the past few days, he'd learned that she did everything on her own time schedule. Listening to him, or better still, forgiving him, weren't in the scope of her composure at the moment.

Possibly not ever.

Way to go, Specialist, he thought with a bitter grin as he glared at the pocketwatch in his bleeding hand. *Mission accomplished.*

14

"LEAVING SO SOON, DEAR?" Norah asked as Emma handed over her room key. "I thought you'd planned to stay through the weekend."

Emma swallowed. She couldn't tell her hostess the truth, that there was no longer any point in staying. "Something's come up," she said vaguely.

Norah printed out her receipt and indicated where Emma should sign. "Well, we're sorry to hear that. If you're ever back in the area, we do hope you'll stay with us again."

It was unlikely that she'd ever be back in the area and she was years away from being able to afford to stay there again—unless someone else was picking up the tab, anyway—but that was hardly worth mentioning. Emma merely smiled and waited for her receipt.

If she wouldn't have had to wake Norah up last night, chances are she would have packed her bags and left right after Payne had walked out of her room. That's what she'd wanted to do, because knowing that he was next door had been utterly excruciating.

Whatever Emma might have expected of him, his cheating at his own rules hadn't been it. In fact, she hadn't been able to decide which had been the greater betrayal—that he'd found the watch and had failed to tell her, or that he'd automatically assumed the worst from her when she'd confronted him with his own duplicity.

Did you go through my pockets?

Mr. Impassive might have mastered hiding his thoughts from everyone else, but for reasons she couldn't begin to explain—a twisted act of fate, she imagined—she'd never had any problem peering into that frighteningly pragmatic mind.

She wasn't about to tell him she'd accidentally kicked his pants when she'd walked back to the bedroom from the bathroom, and the pocketwatch he'd told her that he didn't believe existed had come sailing out of his pocket.

She'd been so stunned—so shocked and hurt—that it had taken every iota of willpower she possessed not to hurl right there on the spot. Brian Payne, a man she'd come to respect because his honor was such an integral part of his personality, had lied to her.

Actually, it was the same sort of lie of omission that she'd employed when she first met him, but now that she was on the receiving end of one, she couldn't say that she altogether appreciated the difference.

Subtle, hell.

A lie was a lie, no matter how one tried to spin it.

He'd said that he'd found the watch last night, but she couldn't imagine when. And, considering that he hadn't told her about it, she had no way of knowing if that was the truth or not. He'd seemed sincere enough, but then she never imagined that he'd have found it and kept it from her to start with. This was precisely the sort of pointless circle her brain had been spinning in all night long, and between the headache it had given her and the heartache compliments of Major Payne, Emma was feeling pretty damned bruised at the moment.

She'd watched him lump her into the same category as those money-grubbing stepmothers he'd had—a little tidbit he'd shared over the course of the past few days—and she'd been so devastated by the unfair comparison that it had been all she could do not to cry. Thankfully, anger had saved her long enough to keep the flood back, but the instant she'd gotten him out of her room, Emma had dropped her head against the door and the let the gates of her despair open.

Dropping that pocketwatch—her future—back into his lap had been the proudest and most disappointing moment in her life, one she imagined would ultimately define her. She wouldn't have taken the damned thing—despite rumors to the contrary, she *was not* ruthless and had fully believed that Payne had known that, too.

Clearly she'd been wrong.

But letting it go—knowing what it was costing her—had been pretty damned hard, also. Emma inhaled a bracing breath and accepted her receipt from Norah.

Regardless, Payne had won fair and square— he'd put his hand on it first and he was rightly entitled to it. She didn't know what he owed Garrett, but she hoped like hell it was worth it. He'd betrayed her trust and broken her heart in the process.

Emma murmured a distracted thanks to Norah, then turned to go.

"Oh, wait!" Norah said. "I've got something for you."

For her? Emma thought. What? More cookies?

She brightened marginally, thinking she could use a little sugar therapy.

"Brian Payne checked out early this morning, as well, but left this for you." She grabbed an envelope from beneath the desk and handed it to her. "He told me to make sure that you got it and I'm such a ninny, I almost let you walk out of here without it." Embarrassed, she shook her head.

Emma's heart jolted into an irregular rhythm. Payne had left her something? She accepted the envelope with slightly shaking hands and knew from the uneven weight that it held Robert E. Lee's pocketwatch. Her mouth parched and little spots danced before her gritty eyes, forcing her to sit down in the nearest wing chair near the door.

She carefully opened the envelope, confirmed that the watch was in there, then pulled out a note that he'd left for her. His crisp masculine scrawl filled a little piece of paper she recognized from the pad in her room.

Emma,
Sorry's inadequate, but I hope that you'll believe me when I say that I'd intended for you to find the watch all along. I knew you'd never let me pay you for it without actually

finding it first—your word was worth more than my money, right?—but that had been my plan, such as it was.

You needed to prove that you could find it first and you needed the money. I don't begrudge you that or think any less of you for wanting it, despite the way it might have appeared last night.

I merely needed the watch, but it's not worth what it's cost me.

Take it and start vet school, and always know that I never intended to hurt you.

Yours,

Payne

P.S. Matilda was wearing the damned thing last night. That's how I found it. Evidently Judith had been at the estate sale, but her name hadn't been on our list. I thought you might have been wondering....

Matilda had been wearing it? Emma thought, astounded. The pig? She thought back, remembered seeing the top hat and tuxedo and...and a pocketwatch. *That's* what he'd hung around for. He hadn't wanted to talk to Matthew—he'd wanted to talk to Judith and get a look at that watch. And he'd wanted her to find it first, then he'd planned to buy it from her? Emma paused, considering.

If she *had* found it first, *had* proven herself, then she imagined she would have allowed him to buy it from her. She would have won the bet for Hastings, would have had the money from Payne to reimburse Hastings for initial payment, as well as the amount she needed to get started in school. Payne would have had the pocketwatch to present to Garrett and everyone would have been happy.

Even Payne, who would have plunked down thousands of dollars simply to be able to hand the watch over to Garrett.

Though she'd tried to worm it out of him, Payne had never told her what he owed Garrett. But it had to be something substantial to go to all of this trouble. Trouble he could have avoided by simply finding the watch himself and moving on. What on earth would prompt him to—

"You look startled, dear," Norah said, concern lining her brow. "Is something wrong?"

Distracted, Emma looked up and shook her head.

Norah paused, seeming to be trying to make up her mind about something. Then she said, "I was surprised to see Mr. Payne this morning. He'd indicated last night after the ghost stories that he'd intended to lengthen his stay and that he had a favor to ask of me. It was odd," she remarked, frowning. "You two seemed to be getting along so well." She offered a kind smile. "I hope you didn't have a falling out. Love's too precious to squander on petty fights."

He'd planned to stay? And he'd wanted Norah's help? He'd never told her that he wasn't leaving this morning. Of course, he'd never really gotten the chance, she conceded, remembering why. *Hot kisses, tangled sighs, naked flesh and bone-wringing orgasms...* Her belly clenched with remembered heat and her nipples tingled behind her bra. Merely thinking about him almost set her off and he was halfway to Atlanta by now, Emma thought, going home empty handed when he could have had it all.

She carefully refolded the letter and slipped it back into the envelope, then stood on legs that weren't altogether steady. She couldn't accept this, Emma decided. Did she appreciate it? Yes. Did she love Brian Payne? More than anything.

But whatever this was costing him had to be more than she stood to lose.

"Have a safe trip back to Marble Springs," Norah said.

"Thanks, I will," Emma told her, smiling. Right after she detoured to Fort Benning and delivered the pocketwatch to Colonel Garrett.

If Payne wouldn't do it, then she would.

Atlanta

"WHERE'S PAYNE?" Jamie asked.

Guy frowned, looked up from the surveillance report he'd been studying. "Same place he's been ever since he came home yesterday afternoon. The Tower."

In a completely uncharacteristic move, Payne had come directly home from the airport, bypassed the office without so much as a status report and taken the elevator upstairs. Guy had called to check in on him, but Payne had gone into lockdown mode and hadn't wanted to talk. He'd kindly told his friend to butt out and Guy had thought it prudent, given the ominous tone in his friend's voice, to take that advice.

Then again, when did he ever do the prudent thing? He stood, cocked his head toward the elevator. "Let's go talk to him."

Jamie gave him a you're-shittin'-me look. "Storm the Tower?"

Guy nodded. "Something's wrong. This isn't like him."

"Didn't he tell you to butt out?"

Guy blinked innocently. "He did. What's your point?" He depressed the call button, waited on the elevator doors to slide open, then selected Payne's floor.

Jamie grimaced, but followed him anyway. "I've got a bad feeling about this," he said, cocking his head at a skeptical angle.

"I do, too," Guy told him. "If he's gotten into the whiskey, then we know we're in trouble."

Payne wasn't much of a recreational drinker, but he had been known to hit the liquor hard when he found something particularly disturbing. He'd gotten dog-ass drunk when his mother had married a guy half her age several years ago—a marriage which had promptly ended in a nasty divorce six months later—and had gotten even drunker still when Danny had died. Payne thrived on being in control, which is why Guy suspected his friend rarely drank. Occasionally, though, something would happen which would force him to let go and *feel* like a normal human being and when that happened, he typically turned to alcohol for help.

If he was drinking, it could only mean one of

two things—he'd either lost the bet and come home without the pocketwatch, or Emma Langsford had gotten under his skin.

Guy grimaced.

Worse still, it could be both.

Jamie knocked on Payne's door and he and Guy stood in the hall and waited for it to open. Half a minute later, Payne appeared at the door. Looking like death warmed over, he wore a silk robe, which had probably cost more than Guy's entire NASCAR memorabilia collection, and held a bottle of Jim Beam loosely in one hand.

Guy and Jamie shared a significant look.

Oh, hell.

15

PAYNE STARED at Guy and Jamie for a moment, then turned on his heel and walked away, leaving the door open so that they could follow him inside if they so chose.

Which naturally they did, because they were nosy bastards who couldn't leave well enough alone.

"I'm fine," Payne said before they could ask. And it was sort of true. With the help of his good buddy Jim Beam, he'd discovered that he could actually numb himself into feeling absolutely fine. So far it was working out splendidly.

The moment he started to miss Emma, to wonder if he'd done the right thing, if she'd ever forgive him, he merely hefted the bottle to his lips and miraculously, he'd begin to feel better. Honestly, Payne thought, as he strolled back to his recliner, he didn't know why he saved getting drunk for nasty occasions.

Guy snagged the remote control from the coffee table, then lowered himself onto Payne's leather sofa and began to idly channel surf. Jamie, on the other hand, had chosen to stand.

"Things went so badly that you have to drink?" Guy asked.

Hell, that was obvious. Didn't the guy see the friggin' bottle in his hand? Payne felt a smile catch the corner of his mouth. Now that was precisely the sort of smart-assed remark Emma would have made.

"Bad enough," Payne told him, Emma's hurt sugared-violet eyes flashing through his mind.

"If it was that bad, then why the hell didn't you call?" Jamie wanted to know. "We would have helped you."

Payne knew that and he appreciated it, but this was something no one could help him with. After a moment, he smiled without humor and told them so.

Jamie and Guy shared another one of those concerned looks. "Is this an I-didn't-complete-my-mission problem or a woman problem?"

They'd find out eventually, so there was no point in lying about it. "A woman problem."

Guy swore. "Dammit, Payne, I warned you about her. What did she do?"

Payne's bleary gaze bored into his friend's, silently warning him away from laying any blame at Emma's door. "*She* didn't do anything. *She* was great. *I'm* the problem."

Guy scowled. "I don't understand. What do you mean, you're the prob—"

Jamie chuckled, and his knowing gaze sparked with instant knowledge only a guy who was also in love could recognize. "She thawed you," he said, seemingly thunderstruck.

"Thawed him?" Guy repeated, looking completely bewildered. "What the hell are you talking about?"

"Are you blind?" Jamie countered, evidently thrilled that he'd figured it out. "He's fallen for—"

The phone rang, cutting Jamie off before he could finish the thought. Payne had set the answering machine to auto-answer so that he didn't have to deal with any calls and grimaced when Garrett's voice once again sounded through the little speakers. "Payne? Payne? If you're there, pick up." Silence then, "Fine. I'll say what I've got to say here and we'll consider this done. Emma Langsford delivered the pocketwatch to me this morning. She said you'd had something come up, and couldn't—"

Stunned, Payne scrambled for the phone. "What? What did you say?"

"So you are there. Excellent," Garrett said. "Emma delivered the pocketwatch to me this morning. I don't know why you sent her, but in any case, *well done.*" His voice brimmed with delight. "I knew you wouldn't fail me. I've wanted this piece forever and thanks to you, I've got it. I know that you think I'm a bit obsessed but…"

No, he'd only failed *her,* Payne thought as Garrett continued to drone on into his ear. He'd doubted her. Why in God's name had she taken Garrett the watch? Why hadn't she given the bloody thing to Hastings and collected her reward? Had she lost her freakin' mind? Payne wondered. What on earth would possess her to do something so reckless? So irresponsible? So noble?

He reeled from the shock of her selflessness and his aching heart expanded painfully in his chest when the gravity of her sacrifice sunk in.

She'd done this for him.

Without even knowing why, Payne realized. Because he'd never told her about Danny's death, about Garrett's favor and his own screwed up connection between the two. She'd given him the benefit of the doubt and had had enough faith in him that she'd been willing to sacrifice her own happiness without knowing what would bring about his.

He didn't know when anything, if ever, had touched him more.

"—at any rate, Major, I truly appreciate this. We're even," he said, and though it could have been simply wishful thinking on his part, Payne felt as though a choke hold had been taken off his neck.

Debt paid. Honor intact. Mission accomplished.

Only now he had one more. Payne stood. "Which one of you bastards is driving me to Marble Springs?"

Guy blinked. "What's in Marble Springs?" Jamie asked, gaping.

With a resigned smirk, Guy fished his keys out of his front pocket. "It's not what, but who," he said, studying Payne as though seeing him for the first time. "I will," he volunteered, "because *this* I've got to see."

Jamie scowled. "I want to go, too."

"Too bad. You have to stay here with your pregnant wife."

"She can come, too. Hell, she's only pregnant. It's not like she's incapacitated."

"This is not a friggin' soap opera," Payne snapped. "This is my life."

Guy grinned. "You're right. It's *better* than a soap opera. We'll wait in the car."

"YOU'RE USING way too many flowers," Darcy snapped. "How many times do I have to tell you, Emma? More greenery, less flowers." She rolled her eyes as though Emma was a complete idiot. "It's basic economics."

No, it was cheap, Emma thought, biting her tongue. Darcy could hang on to more of her easily earned cash if she filled an arrangement full of less-expensive greenery and hoarded more flowers. Unfortunately, she had the market cornered in Marble Springs and people allowed her to get away with it.

But Emma wasn't here to debate Darcy's poor business practices, she was here to work. Money was money and, if she ever wanted to start vet school, Emma needed it. Work was hard to find in her little hometown and she couldn't afford to thumb her nose at the opportunity to make some cash just because the woman paying her was a certified bitch who delighted in making her feel like a second-class citizen.

Welcome to my life, Emma thought, her lips sliding into a wry smile.

Her mother had a hard time grasping this thought process, but oddly she hadn't had a problem with Emma's giving the pocketwatch to the wrong colonel and essentially flushing ten grand down the commode.

That she'd understood.

"I don't know who this man is, honey, but I know if you're willing to make this sort of sacrifice, he has to be worth it."

Evidently love was a universal language and any person who'd ever been in it recognized the dialect when they saw it.

Emma had been glad that her mother understood, because frankly, she didn't think she could have withstood the disappointment if she hadn't. She felt like she was broken inside and the only thing holding her together was her skin.

Hastings hadn't been thrilled with the outcome either, but Emma had held her ground. Payne had found it first. He'd won. Hastings had roared and complained, but he'd been too honorable to demand his money back. The initial payment and expenses had never been contingent upon her winning—that had been her price to make the trip in the first place.

And Garrett, of course, had been delighted. He'd been slightly confused by her arrival, but had ultimately been so beside himself for getting the watch that he hadn't cared who'd delivered it. Emma had desperately wanted to ask him about Payne's terms—what he stood to gain—but didn't.

In the end, it didn't matter.

Whatever his debt, it had been paid and Emma had insisted that Garrett let Payne know that. Not for her sake, but for his own.

God, how she missed him. She ached so much that it hurt to breathe, and more than once over the past couple of days she'd considered calling him, but didn't. If and when the time ever came that he wanted to see her, she was certain he'd let her know. The ball was squarely back in his court.

Emma heard the bell above the door ring, indicating that a customer had walked into the store. She started forward, but Darcy shot her a quelling look. "You just keep working. *I'll* get it."

The implication being that she was too stupid to wait on a customer. Emma gritted her teeth and imagined enrolling in school. That was the goal here, dammit. She could take a little abuse if it meant she'd ultimately have the life she wanted, the one she knew deep in her heart that she deserved.

"Well, good afternoon," Darcy said, and Emma recognized it as her there's-a-good-looking-man-in-my-store kind of voice. God, the woman was such a bitch, Emma thought with a mental eyeroll.

"I'm looking for Emma Langsford."

Payne? she thought faintly.

"Emma?" Darcy asked, as though she couldn't quite believe that Payne would be looking for her.

"Her mother said I'd find her here."

Seemingly drawn forward by the mere sound of his voice, Emma walked out of the back room and paused at the door. Her silly heart lightened and her palms tingled.

Payne's gaze instantly found hers. Those wintry blue eyes were a bit bloodshot and tortured, and she watched a relieved sigh leak from his lips. It was gut-wrenching. "Hiding from me again, I see. I thought I warned you about that."

Emma moved cautiously forward. "What are you doing here?"

"I came for you," he said simply.

Darcy's wide-eyed gaze bounced between them, but Emma ignored her.

"For me?"

Payne cast a hesitant glance at Darcy, then his gaze tangled with hers once more. "Is there somewhere we can talk?"

"She's working right now," Darcy piped up, smirking spitefully. "You'll have to talk to her on your own time, I'm afraid."

Payne turned the full force of his frosty displeasure upon Darcy and she actually backed up a step. "This *is* my own time," he told her. "And I didn't spend the last six hours in the car listening to my friends torment me for falling in love—and having to stop half a dozen times to accommodate a pregnant woman whose bladder has shrunk to the size of a pea—merely to be turned away by you. I'm talking to her *now*. She quits."

"What?" Emma asked, startled by the whole falling-in-love comment. And she quits? she thought faintly, reeling. What the hell was he doing?

"You're not working for her anymore. Get your things. We're leaving."

"Payne—"

"Get them," he repeated.

Of all the high-handed nerve, Emma thought, but couldn't muster any proper outrage. Only an idiot would find Payne's bossy nature on her behalf so damned thrilling, but she did. Her heart did a little loop-de-loop. Truth be told, she was damned turned on, as well. Emma hurried to the back, got her purse, then turned and shot Darcy a self-satisfied smile as Payne held the door open for her.

The look on Darcy's face was priceless.

"Do you want that store?" Payne asked the instant they were outside.

"What?"

"Do you want it? I'll buy it in a heartbeat and put her wicked ass to work for you. God, your mother was right. She *is* a bitch." He glared at her. "How could you take the damned pocketwatch to Garrett and come back to this?" he demanded. "I left it for you so that you wouldn't have to."

"What?" Emma retorted. "Think you've got the market cornered on nobility? You needed it more than I did."

"What on earth made you think that?" Payne demanded.

"You did."

He blinked. "What? How?"

"Payne, I knew it had to be important to you. You don't do anything without a purpose and when I saw all the trouble you'd gone through—all the money you were willing to let go of—simply to be able to hand that watch over to Garrett, I knew it had to be something…significant." She swallowed, huddled deeper into her jacket. "You weren't doing it for the money. Something else had driven you and even though you never told me, it didn't make it any less important."

Payne looked away and a muscle jumped in his tense jaw. "When Danny died, I wanted out of the military," he said. "I didn't care what the cost, I just wanted out. *Needed* to be out."

Emma nodded. "I can see that," she said, aching for him. His pain was palpable, rolling off him in waves that were washing over her and pulling her closer to him.

"Garrett made that happen, and all he asked for in return was a favor." He laughed bitterly. "It was the last tie, you see? The final thing left on my to-do list…and then it would be over. I could fulfill the obligation and start working on my own guilt."

Emma's chest tightened. *"Payne,"* she said, cradling his dear face into her hands. "You have nothing to feel guilty about."

He closed his eyes. "My tactics are what got my friend killed, Emma. I failed and he paid the ultimate price."

Sweet God, she hadn't expected this. Guilt had eroded that legendary logic. "I don't know what happened on this mission. I don't know why your friend died. But I do know you, Payne, and I know that you are The Specialist. The chances of you making a mistake that would have purposely cost your friend his life—would have put his life in any more danger than you and the rest of your unit— are slim to none. Did you do everything to the best of your ability?"

He nodded. "Wasn't good enough."

"Was the mission a success?"

"Yes."

"Was it worthy?"

He swallowed, nodded.

"Then you didn't fail. You just lost a friend in the process."

Payne's wintry blue gaze caught and held hers and the intensity she saw there made her breath catch. "I can't lose you. It would— I can't— I'm in love with you, Emma."

Emma's eyes watered and a light winging sensation took flight in her chest. "I love you, too."

"Kiss her already!"

Startled, Emma glanced at the big SUV parked at the curb. Guy McCann, Jamie Flanagan and a petite dark-haired woman—Jamie's wife, she imagined—were all watching them avidly from the comfort of the warm car. "Shut up," Payne yelled back, exasperated.

He lifted her straight off the pavement, then planted a long, slow kiss on her lips. A tightly braided strand of longing, love and desire wound its way through her and a giddy laugh bubbled up her throat.

"Don't ever leave me again," Payne growled, smiling softly. "It's insulting."

Epilogue

"HOW WAS SCHOOL?" Payne called from the kitchen.

Emma hung her backpack on the peg next to the door and followed the scent of marinated vegetables and grilled chicken. The Tower—her new home—was equipped with top-of-the-line equipment and she imagined she was one of the only students in her class who got to come home to a fabulous meal cooked by a badass former Ranger…in a Kiss the Cook apron.

She chuckled and shook her head. "Where did you get that?" Emma asked.

"Where do you think? Your mother sent it."

Emma chuckled. "She's grateful." In addition to paying off the mortgage, Payne had bought This Bud's For You and put Darcy Marcus to work for her mother. Needless to say, Lena was thrilled. It's what her mother liked to refer to as poetic justice. Emma was just thankful.

"You've fixed a lot," she commented, noting there was enough food to feed an army, or at least a small former part of one.

"Guy, Jamie and Audrey are coming up. Jamie and Audrey are down from Maine. They flew in this morning. I hope you don't mind."

Emma shook her head. "Not at all." She sidled forward and slid her arms around Payne's waist. She pressed a kiss against his chest.

"What are you doing?"

"What the apron says."

Payne growled low in his throat, bent his head and found her mouth. Fire licked through her veins and a bubble of desire burst in her belly, sending whorls of heat swirling through her.

"Geez, don't you guys ever stop?" Guy remarked, strolling in.

Emma chuckled and Payne shot his friend an annoyed look. "Don't you ever knock?"

"I did." He smiled, rather weakly. "Evidently when your fiancée puts her tongue in your mouth, you go deaf."

"It's a talent," Emma told him. "Maybe someday you'll find a girl who can make you go deaf, as well."

Guy rolled his eyes, grimaced. "Let's hope not."

Payne studied his friend. "You're in an uncommonly foul mood. What's wrong?"

Guy collapsed onto the couch, tilted his head back and sighed. "I just got off the phone with Garrett. It's my turn."

Payne stilled. "What does he want?"

Guy shot Payne a droll look. "He wants me to do a special trust-building session for special forces teams at Fort Benning in a couple of weeks," he drawled.

Emma looked at Payne to gauge his response. "So it's not as bad as you thought, then."

Guy looked up and his unreadable troubled gaze connected with Payne's. "You think?"

"You're not guarding a granddaughter or going on a treasure hunt," Payne said, shrugging as though he didn't follow.

"No." He smirked. "I'm just going back into the military." He said it as though it were the equivalent of a death sentence.

A look of communication passed between them, then understanding dawned and Emma inwardly winced for Guy. She cast Payne a sympathetic glance and he squeezed her fingers.

Garrett might have sentenced Jamie to an unethical errand, Payne to a degrading one, but he

was sending Guy McCann right back into the
very place he'd never wanted to be again—the
military…and his own personal hell.

* * * * *

*There's only one bachelor left…and he's about
to meet his downfall.
Don't miss* The Maverick,
*available next month wherever
Mills & Boon® books are sold.*

Turn the page for a tantalising sneak preview…

The Maverick
by
Rhonda Nelson

LOSING HIS TOUCH, HELL, Colonel Carl Garrett thought, mortified by the vicious rumor. He scowled and watched the antique pocket watch—General Robert E. Lee's no less—suspended from his index finger spin slowly in midair. He hadn't spent the past thirty-three years in the military and received his most recent commendation for meritorious service only to be ushered out to pasture to make way for up-and-coming wannabes, dammit.

Him? Retire?

He was certainly old enough, of course, and his wife periodically asked when he planned to hang up his hat, so to speak, but Garrett simply couldn't wrap his mind around being…useless. No longer being of value. His days were filled with purpose, a noble one he'd been proud of from the first moment he'd entered the service, as a wet-behind-the-ears punk with more attitude than sense. The military had thrashed some sense into him, had given him a goal and a dream and the idea of letting those go, of puttering around his greenhouse or trailing along behind his wife at the grocery store was simply…excruciating for him.

The murmurs and rumors of his imminent retirement—a retirement he neither planned nor wanted—had started immediately following his commendation. In retrospect, Garrett realized now he should have seen it for what it was—a nice career ender, the cherry on top of the sundae.

While he knew he commanded the respect of the majority of his peers, he also knew there were a few people around here who wished that he'd move on and make room for new blood. Naturally, one didn't get to his level without making a few enemies. But the idea of doing that was as out of the question now as it had been the first time the issue of his retiring had come up.

Garrett wasn't finished yet. He still had work to do. And to prove that he was as every bit as sharp as he'd always been, he had something up his sleeve. And that something was sitting right outside his office—impatiently, of course, and most likely annoyed and bitter as hell—right this very minute. The thought drew a smile, one of few he'd managed over the past few weeks.

Guy McCann—his maverick.

In all of his years in service, Garrett had never met a man with better instincts and the balls to follow them, no matter how risky the move might be. And when it came to instilling confidence and leading a team, Guy McCann had been the best of the best. He'd led Project Chameleon, one of the most respected covert operation special forces units the army had ever known, on more than two dozen highly dangerous missions—and had been successful each and every time, an unparalled record.

His days of service were over, of course, but if McCann could teach this new team Garrett had put together a fraction of the skill he possessed, then that would put an end to the rumors that he'd lost his touch.

The proof was in the pudding, so to speak, and Garrett was counting on McCann to whip up something special.

Given McCann's present state of mind, it might not be the most prudent move for Garrett to put his faith in the troubled former Ranger. But like McCann, there were times when a man simply had to follow his instincts, and each and every one of Garrett's told him that McCann needed to fulfill this favor just as much as Garrett needed him to be successful.

Garrett scowled, thinking of the coming confrontation. It was a pity they were about to get off to such a bad start.

THE ROYAL HOUSE OF NIROLI

...International affairs, seduction and passion guaranteed

Volume 1 – July 2007
The Future King's Pregnant Mistress by Penny Jordan

Volume 2 – August 2007
Surgeon Prince, Ordinary Wife by Melanie Milburne

Volume 3 – September 2007
Bought by the Billionaire Prince by Carol Marinelli

Volume 4 – October 2007
The Tycoon's Princess Bride by Natasha Oakley

8 volumes in all to collect!

THE ROYAL HOUSE OF NIROLI

*...International affairs, seduction
and passion guaranteed*

Volume 5 – November 2007
Expecting His Royal Baby by Susan Stephens

Volume 6 – December 2007
The Prince's Forbidden Virgin by Robyn Donald

Volume 7 – January 2008
Bride by Royal Appointment by Raye Morgan

Volume 8 – February 2008
A Royal Bride at the Sheikh's Command by Penny Jordan

8 volumes in all to collect!

0807/009/MB103

Mediterranean Men

Let them sweep you off your feet!

Gorgeous Greeks

The Greek Bridegroom by Helen Bianchin
The Greek Tycoon's Mistress by Julia James
Available 20th July 2007

Seductive Spaniards

At the Spaniard's Pleasure by Jacqueline Baird
The Spaniard's Woman by Diana Hamilton
Available 17th August 2007

Irresistible Italians

The Italian's Wife by Lynne Graham
The Italian's Passionate Proposal by Sarah Morgan
Available 21st September 2007

2 FREE

BOOKS AND A SURPRISE GIFT!

We would like to take this opportunity to thank you for reading this Mills & Boon® book by offering you the chance to take TWO more specially selected titles from the Blaze® series absolutely FREE! We're also making this offer to introduce you to the benefits of the Mills & Boon® Reader Service™—

> ★ **FREE home delivery**
> ★ **FREE gifts and competitions**
> ★ **FREE monthly Newsletter**
> ★ **Exclusive Reader Service offers**
> ★ **Books available before they're in the shops**

Accepting these FREE books and gift places you under no obligation to buy, you may cancel at any time, even after receiving your free shipment. Simply complete your details below and return the entire page to the address below. You don't even need a stamp!

YES! Please send me 2 free Blaze books and a surprise gift. I understand that unless you hear from me. I will receive 4 superb new titles every month for just £3.10 each, postage and packing free. I am under no obligation to purchase any books and may cancel my subscription at any time. The free books and gift will be mine to keep in any case.

K7ZED

Ms/Mrs/Miss/Mr ....Initials ....

BLOCK CAPITALS PLEASE

Surname ....

Address ....

....

....Postcode..................................

Send this whole page to:
UK: FREEPOST CN81, Croydon, CR9 3WZ